A VERY FUMBLING MERRY CHRISTMAS

EVA HAINING

Copyright

Also By Eva Haining

Manhattan Knights Series
Flawless
Relentless
Endless
Complete Manhattan Knights Series Box Set

Mustang Ranch Series
Mustang Daddy
Mustang Buck
Mustang Hollywood
Mustang Christmas
Mustang Belle
Mustang Player

Hall of Fame Series
Fumble
A Very Fumbling Merry Christmas
Interception
Screwball
Strike Zone

Chapter 1
FAITH

I'VE ALWAYS LOVED THANKSGIVING. What's not to love about a day filled with family, food, and football? This year I'm taking over the mantle for the Fairchild Family Thanksgiving meal. My dad is thawing a little toward Hunter and me as a couple, so I jumped at the opportunity to have the entire family to our new home. My grandparents arrived last night, and my Grams has been shamelessly flirting with Hunter since she stepped through the door.

Papa parked himself in an armchair in front of the television and fell asleep listening to the news a few hours ago. My mom and dad are driving up tonight with my brother, Ben, and his wife. It's going to be interesting, to say the least. Ben wasn't exactly my biggest fan when my relationship with Hunter sort of overshadowed his wedding a few months back.

I'm hoping this holiday season will be a good chance to get back to some kind of normalcy with my folks. It's a little daunting to be hosting my first family holiday a month after getting married, but I'm jumping in with both feet.

My stomach is churning with nerves, so I busy myself with food preparation for tomorrow and pour myself a generous glass of Prosecco. Hunter spies me out of the corner of his eye, chugging my drink like it's Gatorade. Excusing himself from my Grams' clutches, he saunters over to me, leaning against the kitchen island with the easy grace I adore. *If only I were blessed with a modicum of his elegance.*

"Slow down there, slugger. You'll be slurring your words before Coop and Zee get here if you keep slinging it back." He eyes me warily, reading my mind.

"This all seemed like a great idea last week. Now I'm thinking it's going to be a disaster." He reaches out, grabbing me around the waist and pulling me close to his chest.

"You're probably right. It's going to be a shitshow." My shoulders sag as his deep chuckle vibrates through me.

"Why did you let me do this?"

"When have I ever *let* you do anything? You're a one-woman wrecking ball... and I love you. You're stubborn as hell. I'm not telling you to do or not do something." His hands rub up and down my back, calming me as I sink into his embrace.

"Promise you'll still love me after the holidays, no matter how crazy it gets?"

"Love, you already know the answer to that. You can't get rid of me that easily. A bad family dinner is no big deal in the scheme of things. This is our first Thanksgiving. That already makes it amazing."

"Smooth talker."

"You know it." I take a moment to breathe him in, steeling myself for tomorrow. I lean in for a kiss, losing myself for a few precious seconds of quiet in what I know will be a storm.

"Y'all are so cute. Back in the day, your grandfather used to ravage me anywhere and everywhere. Still gives me butterflies after all these years." She looks over to my grandpa, snoring in the chair in front of the television.

"Aw, Grams, I love that. I hope we're like that when we're old."

"Faith Fairchild, are you calling me old?" She feigns offense and winks at me while Hunter isn't looking.

"If it's any consolation, Mrs. Fairchild, she calls me old on a daily basis. And she's Faith Vaughn now. I claimed her. Filled out the marriage license and everything!" I love that he's being playful with her.

"You're still a fetus, Hunter. Trust me... I'm old!"

"Well, I appreciate that, ma'am."

"None of that ma'am business. You call me Constance. Now, don't let me interrupt you young lovebirds any longer. I'm going to go and have a little nap while your grandfather snores out here. Honestly, it's like sleeping next to a freight train."

I go to Grams' side, all conspiratorial as we tiptoe past Grandpa. She and I have always been kindred spirits. We have the same little rebellious streak. As we make our way to her room, she holds me a little tighter.

"You've got yourself a good man there, Faithy. He looks at you the same way your grandpa looked at me all those years ago."

"Really?" I don't know why I need her validation. I guess it's nice that one member of the Fairchild family doesn't think Hunter is too old for me. I didn't wake up one day and think, *I'm going to go and fall in love with an older man.* I didn't plan to fall in love at all this year. Hunter was supposed to be an introduction to sex. It already feels inconceivable that I believed I could sleep with him and then walk away without any emotional ties.

Grams takes a seat on the edge of the bed and pats the mattress for me to sit with her.

"When I first met your grandpa, he was the most handsome man I'd ever met. I couldn't stop thinking about him." The warmth of her smile as she reminisces is so adorable. "Do you know, the day we met, he told his best friend that he was going to marry me?"

"That's true love."

"I didn't know he was 'the one' for a good while after we started dating. In fact, I was planning on him being a fling, but... oh my word... the things that man could do to me in bed."

"Grams!" I stop her before she says anything else. No one needs to hear their grandmother talk sex.

"Oh, don't you give me that, Faith Fairchild. Actually, Faith

Vaughn now, I suppose. Don't you go telling me to shush. I watch the news. I saw your antics with that husband of yours. Sex is part of life. If it weren't for your grandpa rocking my world, your daddy wouldn't be here, and you wouldn't exist. I enjoy sex as much as the next woman. The day I die will be the day I stop having sex."

"Oh my God! Grams, please stop saying the word sex."

"Sex, sex, sex!"

"Okay, I'm leaving now." I jump up and overexaggerate my reaction. I know she'll get a kick out of it. I give her a conspiratorial wink as I head for the door, but she stops me in my tracks.

"Faith."

"Yeah?"

"Don't ever apologize for loving him or for being loved by him. Finding your soulmate isn't a guarantee in this life. You hit the jackpot. Don't let your dad or anyone else take a moment of your joy."

Her words hit me right in the feels.

"Thanks, Grams."

"Now scram, I need to get that nap in before your grandpa comes in and snores in my ear!"

As I head back out to the living room, I think about what she said. I found my soulmate. Hunter is standing at the kitchen island, his eyes fixed on me with a heart-stopping smile on his face. Gazing at him now, I look forward to the days, months, and years ahead of us. New adventures that we get to share with each other and this holiday season is going to be the start of so many wonderful memories we make together.

Let's just hope we can get through Thanksgiving dinner without my dad trying to sucker- punch my husband.

I have been up since the crack of dawn, and that means so has everyone else. A colossal crash at five o'clock scared the crap out of me and made me squeal like a maniac. I was trying to pull out a baking tray without having to move everything else around, so obviously, every pot and pan we own ended up tumbling out of the cabinet and onto the floor of our kitchen. I'm amazed I didn't break anything. A string of expletives later, and everyone was awake with a bang.

Unfortunately, Hunter didn't think to throw on some clothes before he came rushing out to check on me. When my dad came running down the hall, he was welcomed by the sight of me crouched next to Hunter in a rather compromising position, and my delicious husband had on nothing but a pair of boxers. It wouldn't be a big deal considering I'm sure my dad has seen Hunter walking around naked in the locker room more times than he could count, but this was far worse. I can't help myself when it comes to Hunter. I just had to lean in for that kiss and run my hand over his wash-board abs. He quickly extricated himself from my grasp and suggested I put on the coffee machine while he cleaned up the mess, and then he disappeared for a few minutes to shrug on a t-shirt and some sweats.

By the time he reemerged, my dad and I were busy getting the turkey ready to go in the oven, and I could see that Hunter didn't want to interrupt our time together. It's been hard for both of us. Although my dad came to the wedding, things have still been a little rocky ever since. My mom, on the other hand, has rolled with the tide and embraced Hunter as an official member of the family.

Zoey has been the MVP of the day. Any lulls or hesitations, she's on it. When I've backed myself into an uncomfortable spot, she and Coop just breeze on past and change the topic of conversation.

I'm not one to judge—people who live in glass houses springs to mind—but they make an odd pair at times. Although they are much closer in age than Hunter and I, Zoey is definitely the more mature between them. Coop is a walking billboard for an NFL star at the top of his game—not necessarily the most mature person on the planet, but his playful personality draws you in. He and Hunter are like brothers, and that makes me love him. I'm a little worried at what this all looks like if he and Zee don't work out.

Zoey is family to me. She's stuck by me through thick and thin without judgment. I don't think I could've gotten through this year without her. There's always going to be a seat at my dinner table for her during the holidays, but by the same token, I know Hunter would say the same about Coop. I'm just crossing my fingers, eyes, arms, and legs, hoping beyond hope that they are the real deal. If not, the most I can hope for is a friendly breakup.

With the table set and everyone taking their seats, I'm too nervous to enjoy the meal I've been slaving over since sunrise. Zee and Coop are already joking around with Grams, and she, in turn, is being the quirky little minx I know and love. My dad just rolls his eyes at his mom's antics. She's always been more laid-back than him. Thankfully, I know he'll cheer up when he starts eating. Dad is one of those 'hangry' people. If you leave him hungry, his mood deteriorates at a rapid rate! I've made all of his favorites.

Hunter helps me get all of the food-filled dishes along the center of the table without incident, and when I reach for the turkey platter, he comes running to my side.

"Let me get that for you. I love you, but if you fall over yourself, and this amazing-looking turkey takes a nosedive, I won't be responsible for my actions." He gives me a chaste kiss and a sly wink.

"Are we talking punishment? I might have to throw the game on purpose." Wiggling my eyebrows at him, he shakes his head and leans in close to my ear so only I can hear.

"If you're lucky, I might just bend you over our bed later. You look so fucking hot in that dress." His words send a thrill through me and straight to my core.

"I'll hold you to that, Mr. Vaughn."

"I'm counting on it, Mrs. Vaughn." With another chaste kiss, he adjusts himself to hide the semi he's sporting right now. When he's ready, he picks up the platter and carries it over to the table as if it were a rare and fragile gift. It's exciting to hear everyone ooh and aah over it. I can't help but think of Dr. Seuss as I hand the carving knife to Hunter.

"Are you ready to carve the roast beast?" As he takes the knife from my hand, his fingers brush my skin, a small gesture to calm my nerves.

"This looks amazing, Faith. The whole spread is phenomenal." Everyone nods in agreement, and my heart swells with pride. I take my seat next to him at the head of the table with Zee on my side. She wraps her arm around my shoulder as Hunter slices into the turkey.

"It's not exploding like the one in *National Lampoon's Christmas Vacation*. I'd say that's a win, friend."

"Thanks for the vote of confidence." I chuckle. Zee knows me too well, and she's right. This bird could taste like crap, but it didn't explode. My expectations are low!

As everyone begins to fill their plates, I sit back and take it all in for a moment. My brother and his wife are talking baby names with my parents. Coop is making Grams blush by meeting her shameless flirting with charm and wit. When I look to Hunter, he's staring right back at me.

"Hey, beautiful."

"Hey, yourself." The intensity of his gaze makes my stomach somersault.

"Everyone is enjoying themselves. You did amazing." I reach over and grab his hand, pulling him in for a kiss. The scent of his cologne washes over me, and I lose myself for a moment, holding our kiss a beat longer than I should.

When I pull back, my dad is shaking his head at our PDA. I'm not getting into it with him—not today. My Grams has other ideas.

"You really need to get that stick out of your ass, son." The table goes silent as everyone turns to Grams.

"Excuse me?" My dad looks pissed.

"You heard me just fine. You should be happy your daughter found such an upstanding, successful man. Instead, you look like you swallowed a wasp."

"I just think the dinner table isn't the place for making out." Even my mom rolls her eyes at that pathetic attempt to hide his disdain.

"Oh, hush up. You've always been a prude. I don't know where you get it from. Your father and I have always been so adventurous in the bedroom. Heck, you were conceived in a public restroom off Route 66."

You hear about the color draining from someone's face, but this is the first time I've actually witnessed it. I'm guessing this is new information. My dad looks positively disgusted.

"Stop it, Mother. You're embarrassing yourself."

"Me? I'm not the one getting bent out of shape over a peck on the lips and a few years of an age difference."

"You don't know what you're talking about. Can we just get back to eating?"

"No. We can't. I want to make a toast." My dad watches in abject horror, waiting for Grams to mortify him further. "To Faith and Hunter. Thank you for inviting us to share this delicious Thanksgiving meal with you. Young love should be celebrated, and I, for one, am thankful that you found each other. It has been a joy to see Faithy blossom this year. So, let's all raise a glass to Faith and Hunter. You kids have a lifetime of happy memories, exciting adventures ahead. Be kind to each other, compromise, and never go to bed on an argument."

Everyone raises their glasses, and my dad seems to have been put firmly in his place. Grams can still stare him down when she wants to. Coop decides to take her lead and raises a glass for the things he's grateful for this year. Everyone else follows suit, and when it gets to Hunter, he raises his glass, gesturing toward me.

"To my beautiful Faith. I always thought the NFL would be the highlight of my life. When I busted my knee, I thought my best days were behind me. I thought I'd never replace the elation of being on the field with thousands of fans cheering my name. I thought it was all downhill the day my playing career ended. How wrong I was.

"The day you stood in front of our friends and family and vowed to be my wife… that was the single greatest moment of my life thus far. This is the first year I have felt truly thankful for the twists and turns my life has taken this year. You came stumbling into my life, literally, and changed my world. You're everything I didn't know I needed. I love you and feel so blessed to be your husband. Thank you for choosing me."

Tears well in my eyes as I take his words to heart. He floors me with his eloquence and that sexy grin of his. Everyone seems moved by his toast, and just when I think we're out of the woods, I hear my

Grams lean into Grandpa and say, "That was a good speech. He's getting lucky tonight."

Coop and Zee burst out laughing, defusing the situation, and just like that, we've survived our first Thanksgiving. And my Grams wasn't wrong—after that toast, Hunter is definitely getting lucky tonight. He'll be stuffing my turkey good and hard!

Chapter 2
HUNTER

TO SAY I'm relieved as we wave goodbye to Faith's family is the understatement of the century. I consider myself a pretty social guy —but fuck me—I was feeling the pressure to impress. It's crazy considering how much time I've spent with all of these people over the years, but there's a huge difference between being a family friend and an in-law.

Coop and Zee are the only two left, which is fine. I don't need to impress them or watch the way I interact with Faith. I've been trying to hold back when it comes to PDA around her family. We didn't exactly have the best start, and shoving it in their faces isn't going to help matters now. It's so hard for me not to touch or kiss her when I want to. It feels unnatural. Coop and Zee don't give a shit, so I'm looking forward to kicking back and sharing a few laughs with them before we get back to work.

December is going to be a little chaotic, but I'm determined to make this festive season memorable for Faith. First Christmas together is a big deal when you're dating someone, but we've done everything at hyper-speed this year. We're married already and experiencing all of these firsts in quick succession.

With my arm wrapped around Faith's shoulder, I pull her close.

"You did great."

"You think?"

"No one got food poisoning, you didn't chop off any fingers, so I'd say that's a win. Your Grams is a riot. Now I see where you get your mischievous streak." She lets out a little chuckle that tells me she already knew that.

As we head into the living room, Coop and Zee are deep in conversation, but the second they see us—radio silence. They've been cagey since they got here. It's not like Coop, and the way Faith speaks about Zoey, it doesn't seem like her either.

"Anyone want another drink?"

"Scotch, straight up," Coop blurts out immediately. Even Faith notices that he's acting strange.

"Put your feet up, love. You've been doing the hostess thing for days. I'll grab you a drink." As she moves to leave my side, I can't help myself, pulling her back for a long-overdue kiss. The scent of her perfume tantalizes my senses, and I forget the past few days of holding back when it comes to her.

I take a few minutes to pour drinks, and when everyone has a glass in hand, I settle down next to Faith.

"Seeing you all domesticated and hanging with the in-laws felt like a harbinger of the apocalypse." Coop throws back his drink before swiping mine and draining it.

"Jealousy doesn't suit you, bro." I should've known to bring Coop a bottle rather than a glass. I stand to go grab the scotch from the kitchen, and Coop follows me like a teenage girl. "We don't go to the restroom in pairs. When did you get a vagina installed?" He grabs me by the arm and drags me out of earshot of the girls.

"How did you know Faith was the one? Does it feel different when you bang her?" I grab the scotch and thrust it so hard against his chest, it sends him stumbling backward.

"If you ever use the word *bang* concerning Faith again, I'll shove this bottle so far up your ass you'll be shitting glass for the rest of your life."

"I'm serious. How did you know?" Coop pins me with an unnervingly serious stare.

"What the hell is going on with you? Is this about Zee?" Realization dawns. "You're in love with her. Holy shit! I never thought I'd see the day."

"I'm not in love with her!" Coop exclaims a little too loud. The second the words leave his lips, he turns to see Zee shaking her head.

"Thanks, Coop. The feeling's mutual," she says, her lack of conviction evident in her tone.

"Babe, I didn't mean that. I mean... I'm not saying I love you. It's way too early for that shit, right?"

"Yep. I'm only dating you for your huge cock and an expensive Christmas present."

Faith sits speechless, her eyes fixed on her best friend. Coop looks a little hurt by her statement but quickly shakes it off.

"I've got you covered on that one. I'm somewhat of a gift-giving savant."

"If I keep you around that long, I'll be the judge of your gifting skills." The tension in the room is tangible. I shoot a quick glance in Faith's direction, nodding my head in Zee's direction. Someone needs to say something, but I have no idea what to say. Thankfully, she knows what I mean.

"I know I'm going to trump Hunter in the gift department." A wry smile tugs at the corner of her lips. She's concocting a plan. The last time she did that, I popped her cherry and then married her.

"Oh really? I highly doubt it. I already have an early Christmas gift for you. Actually, me and Coop have been planning it for weeks." Coop has no idea what I'm about to say, but he has the good sense to stay quiet. Whatever is going on with him and Zee, I figure he could use some brownie points right about now.

"Spill."

"We've organized a romantic getaway for the four of us." I'm making this up as I go. I was planning on taking Faith to a small place I have in Aspen. It was going to be a naked weekend. It's not like I'd take Faith skiing. God, she can't walk in a straight line without falling on her ass. Skiing would be a suicide mission.

"Where? When?" It makes me smile to see how excited she is.

"Aspen. Two weeks from now. Gives us enough time to decorate the house, but not too close to Christmas that we'll miss out on any of the fun stuff. You up for it? Four days of snow, smores, and spiced mulled wine." Faith makes a beeline for me, just about knocking me on my ass when she slams into me.

"Oh my God! I love the snow. It's going to be amazing." Pushing up on to her tiptoes, she nips at my bottom lip, sending a jolt straight to my cock. If Coop and Zee weren't here right now, I'd have my super-hot wife naked on the kitchen island. Fuck it—my lips crash down on hers as my hands fist in her hair, pulling her close. My cock springs to life, pressing against her thigh.

"Maybe it should just be the two of us…" Before I get a chance to finish my sentence, Zoey is yelling in the background.

"We're going to Aspen! You don't get to ditch us now, Vaughn." She turns to Coop and wraps her arms around his neck.

"What's this for?" Coop asks with trepidation.

"Thank you for thinking of me. This is a great surprise." Coop mouths the words, *thank you* as he wraps his arms around his girlfriend. Faith nudges me, knowing exactly what's going on. I put my finger to my lips, begging her to keep quiet. With a genuine smile, she snuggles into me, her hand drifting lower, making its way to where I want her most.

"Keep going, and I'll throw you over my shoulder and take you to our bedroom."

"Promises, promises, Mr. Vaughn." I'm about to lift her when Zee interrupts.

"Y'all can have your sexathon later. Right now, I want all the details of our trip." Fuck, I'm going to have to think fast. I can't tell her that they were never part of the plan. Faith senses my unease and steps in.

"I didn't get to tell you about my great idea yet. Hunter totally stole my thunder." She grabs my hand and drags me over to the couch. I try to adjust my pants, but there's no hiding the tripod I'm sporting right now.

"I can see why you chose Hunter to pop your cherry, girl. You're lucky that monster didn't split you in two."

"Stop checking out my husband's cock, Zee!" I love that Faith's tone is jokey but with a possessive undercurrent.

"In my defense, it's kind of hard to miss right now." Coop's brow furrows, but he keeps his mouth shut, which is so unlike him. Has he been replaced with an alien imposter? This guy has got it bad.

"Secret Santa!" Faith blurts out. She does that sometimes—shouts one or two words that really should be part of a coherent thought. I've gotten used to reminding her that I can't actually read her mind.

"You're going to have to elaborate on that thought, love." I chuckle as she realizes we have no idea what she's talking about.

"Yeah. So, I was thinking you and I could have a little wager." The second I hear the word, I know I'm in for a crazy December.

"Another wager? You know how the last one turned out."

"Exactly! I got the man of my dreams, and I won the wager. You cashed in my V-Card. You really punched it, stamped it, humped it to within an inch of its life." Coop and Zee snigger as Faith goes off on one of her tangents.

"Love, please stop talking about your V-Card. What's the new wager?" I know I'm going to regret asking.

"My favorite part of Christmas was never big or expensive gifts. It was the junk I got in my stocking. The silly games or some little trinket that 'Santa' knew I liked. I think it would be fun to have a Secret Santa wager. From now until Christmas Eve, we see which one of us can find the most ridiculous, funny gift for each other. What do you think?"

God, I love her sense of humor. This is actually a really good idea. It will certainly make the yuletide interesting. Not that it could ever be dull with Faith around. I hold out my hand to shake on it.

"You have yourself a deal, Mrs. Vaughn."

"Oh, hold up!" Zee interjects. "We want in on that wager." Coop looks as surprised as me.

"We do?"

"Come on. We could use some fun! If we're all going to Aspen together, we should all be in on this wager. They got to have so much fun with their last one. Why shouldn't we have some laughs?"

"I thought you weren't sure if you wanted to keep me around until Christmas."

"Don't be a drama queen, Coop. Let's do it, please?" One look at her pouty lips, and he's a goner. They both turn to us expectantly, seeking entrance to another of Faith's hair-brained plans.

"Wasn't my idea. Not my call. What do you think, Faith? It's your hair-brained scheme. Does this plan have room for two more?"

"I'd have gladly helped with the first plan if given the chance." Coop thinks he's being funny, but I want to throat punch him right about now.

"Say that again, and your Christmas present from me will be a shallow grave." Faith is practically bouncing, she's so excited at the prospect of a new game.

"Okay, okay. We can make this work. It's going to be even better with all four of us. First, we need some ground rules."

"We're listening."

"First of all, there's a hundred dollar spend limit for any one gift. Second, you can only gift once a day. Rule three, this is anonymous in the spirit of Secret Santa. We don't have to pick names out of a hat or anything. You're free to gift to whomever you choose. On Christmas Eve, we'll reveal who gave each of the gifts. Sound good?"

Coop immediately chimes in with the same thought as me. "Are we allowed dirty gifts?" Faith looks to me with mischief dancing in her eyes like sugar plum fairies before wiggling her eyebrows suggestively.

"Anything goes!" She's going to be the death of me.

"Are you sure about that? Coop has a pretty twisted sense of humor."

"It'll be fun. Yes, anything goes." Then, I see the light go on in Zee's eyes. She's already thinking up something dirty.

"We need to add another rule. Whatever gift you receive, you *have* to use it." I suddenly feel old as fuck.

"Are you all remembering that I'm an old man pushing forty?"

"All the more fun," Faith teases. I should've kept my mouth shut. Coop is going to crucify me.

"Okay, old man river. I'm going to be in my thirties next year. Is this what I have to look forward to?"

"I could still take you down on and off the field, Danford!"

"I just let you think that. I wouldn't want you to bust a hip trying to keep up with me."

"You're right. I wouldn't want to injure myself walking to the closet to get my Hall of Fame jacket. You don't have that problem." Verbal sparring with Coop is one of my favorite pastimes. Only the three Fs give me more pleasure—Faith, fucking, and football.

Coop flips me the bird before grabbing four shot glasses from the kitchen and a bottle of tequila from my not-so-secret liquor cabinet. Handing us each a shot glass, he fills them to the rim.

"To our festive wager. May Secret Santa bring you everything you want this Christmas, and maybe some stuff you don't. To us... the naughty and the nice!"

Chapter 3
HUNTER

COOP and I throw our shots back, and Faith is hot on our tail. She's going to feel rough in the morning. Zee is the only one who registered the epically bad idea of mixing drinks. She hands her shot to Faith.

"I'm not mixing. Some of us have work on Monday. You know... real jobs and necessary paychecks?" Coop snakes his arms around her waist from behind.

"I'll give you ten grand to blow off work this week." If he could see her face right now, he'd realize he needs to shut the fuck up. "I'll be your sugar daddy." She shrugs out of his arms, less than amused.

"I don't need you to be any kind of daddy, thanks. You might wipe your ass with hundred-dollar bills, but I don't accept handouts." Even Faith looks a little surprised by her outburst.

"I was only kidding. Chill out, Zee. I just... I'll miss you because I have to go back to training on Monday, and I won't see you until our trip. Trust me, I know you're not a gold digger."

"I'm not going to lie, I am happy not to be training on Monday." I attempt to diffuse the situation. Faith follows suit.

"You're going to wish you were back in the locker room after a day of Christmas decoration shopping with me!"

"Do I have to come?"

"It's our first Christmas. We need to pick out decorations that are going to become family heirlooms."

"Doesn't that require an heir to… loom it to?" My brain is suddenly a scrambled mess.

"Calm down. I'm not talking about any time in the near future. God, do you really need to be so male about it?" She's teasing me now, but I hadn't thought about what our family would look like in the near or distant future.

"I will happily go shopping with you and pick out the treasures for future generations of Vaughns." Faith throws her arms around me, planting a heart-stopping kiss on me which I quickly deepen, darting my tongue out to lick the seam of her lips.

"God, you two make me want to barf." There's a little bite in Zee's voice. She's trying to pass it off as playful, but she's pissed about something. Not my girl, not my problem. Coop will need to navigate his own landmines with that one.

"Don't worry, I'm taking him to bed to have my wicked way. That tequila is kicking in, and my husband is about to be wearing my thighs like earmuffs."

Grabbing my hand, Faith drags me down the hall without another word to our friends. I'd tell her it's impolite to leave guests to their own devices, but it's Coop, and I'm about to get lucky, so it's every man for himself.

"Night, guys!" Coop mumbles a 'good night' in our direction before getting into it with Zee. I can just about hear what they're arguing about as Faith closes the door behind us. I'm sure Coop can handle himself just fine. My attention is now completely focused on my wife.

Backing her over to the bed, I reach for the hem of her dress, my hands caressing up her legs.

"What were you saying about earmuffs? Care to elaborate?"

"Consider it your first holiday gift." As my hand reaches the apex of her thighs, I'm surprised by the distinct lack of lace.

"You're not wearing any panties. When did you take them off?"

"I didn't put any on today." Fuck, she is hot when she's being a tease. I caress my fingers over her clit so softly, it's almost a ghost of a touch.

"Why didn't you let me in on this little secret earlier?"

"Because it wasn't for you, it was for me. Knowing that in a room full of people, you had no idea that every kiss, every stolen caress was making me wet for you. I find it sexy to know that my pussy has been ready and waiting for you all day—a torturous pleasure. When your lips brushed mine, I felt it at my core, driving me wild for you."

I have no words for how turned on she makes me. Instead, my lips crash down on hers as I stumble to the bed, throwing her down before dropping to my knees and spreading her legs. The evidence of her arousal has my cock standing at attention, but I plan on enjoying every second and every inch of her body tonight. If she's been anticipating this all day, I'm going to deliver.

I bury my head between her thighs, licking from her entrance to her clit in one long, languorous stroke. She tastes so fucking good, and the way she writhes beneath me is such a turn on. I set a punishing rhythm, worshiping at her altar. When she reaches down and grabs my hair, she forces me to take her—harder—faster—riding my face to an explosive orgasm. She loses herself in the moment, screaming my name. I'm straight-up ready to blow my load at the sight of her.

She lets go of me and shuffles out of her dress. When I think she can't get any sexier, she nods in my direction, her eyes burning a hole through my crotch.

"Lose the clothes, Mr. Vaughn." I'm eager to oblige, but I'm stopped in my tracks as she slides over to the edge of the bed and drops her head over the edge.

"Don't tease me, woman."

"Take your clothes off and get over here. I want to suck your cock. Now." Holy shit. I don't think I've ever undressed so quickly in my life. I practically fall over myself to get out of my pants. My cock is straining, hard as a fucking rock, as I step toward her. I can feel her breath on my skin as I stand just far enough that she can't reach.

"Open that pretty little mouth of yours, sweetheart." Her eyes are alight with desire as she opens her lips, her breath ragged as she waits for me. She looks so fucking hot right now. I love a blow job as much as the next man, but this particular angle is sublime. I wrap my fist around the base of my cock and shift forward, just enough for her to dart her tongue out and lick the tip. It's like a lightning bolt to my already amped-up erection.

I tease myself, edging back and forth, watching as she flicks her tongue, her perfect, pouty lips pressing feather-light kisses to my skin. She looks so damn hot, I can barely tear my eyes away from her lips on my cock, but I want to see every inch of her naked flesh spread out on the bed in front of me. Fuck, I need to calm down before I come in her mouth after thirty seconds of her lips on me. I take a step back, but she's not having it. She reaches out to pull me closer, but she overreaches, pushing herself too far. Her legs fly into the air, and she fumbles to stop herself, but it's too late.

I manage to grab her just before she hits the floor—my graceful wife. With her ass in the air, I wrap my arm around her waist and get her back up on the bed.

"For the love of God! Why can't I do one thing that's actually sexy?" Her cheeks are flushed as she throws her arm up to cover her eyes.

"Are you kidding me? That angle is the single sexiest thing I've ever seen. It's probably good you fell when you did. I was about to shoot my load."

"And then I ruined it."

"You haven't ruined anything. Do you trust me?"

"Yes."

"Then move back to the same position and let me take the lead." A shy smile tugs at the corner of her lips, and I can't wait to feel them wrapped around the raging hard-on I'm still sporting. She does as I ask, positioning her head to where she can drop it back over the edge of the bed. This time, I'm not taking any chances.

When she's right where I want her, I reach out my hands, leaning over to cup her breasts. Trailing my fingers over her nipples and down her stomach, I make sure to keep my cock just out of reach. I want her desperate for me. She arches her back up off the bed as my hands travel lower.

"Hunter! Oh God, yes!" She can't help herself as I caress her folds.

"You need to be quiet, love. We have guests. Do I have to give you something to keep that pretty little mouth of yours silent?"

"Yes." I leave her on the edge of release as I stand to position myself. As she opens her mouth, I let her take as much of me as she can, and fuck, at this angle, that's a whole lot of me. I brace my hands on either side of her for a moment, struggling for composure.

"Wow. Slow down, Faith. I want to savor the sight of you."

I steady myself before letting my hands begin to roam her body, grinding my hips in a lazy rhythm. The wet warmth of her mouth is fucking glorious. When she lets her body relax in the knowledge that I won't let her fall, she submits completely, allowing me to rock in and out, driving me to the brink.

"Spread your legs, Faith. Let me see how slick you are for me." She opens for me without hesitation, a satisfied moan vibrating against my cock as I bend forward and flick my tongue over her clit. She begins to writhe, straining her legs as wide as they'll go. I lavish her with kisses before taking a sharp intake of breath. It creates a cold sensation after the warmth of my mouth on her, and it gets the desired response.

Her hips begin to move to the same rhythm as mine while I thrust my cock deeper and deeper. Wrapping one arm around her thigh, I flick, kiss, and caress her until I know she's close. Only then do I slide two fingers inside of her. She's soaking wet for me. I can't hold back the roar that escapes my chest as she climaxes, her walls tightening around my fingers as my tongue circles her clit, letting her ride out the aftershocks.

The way she's sucking my cock right now, you'd think it was a candy cane. I'm not coming in her mouth. I want to sink balls deep into her and watch her come apart beneath me again.

It's torturous to pull my cock from her lips, but I'm quick to pull her around until her legs are hanging over the bed.

"Why did you stop? You haven't finished."

"Exactly. I'm not done with you, Faith. Wrap your legs around my waist." I stand at the edge of the bed, positioning my cock at her entrance before hammering into her with one long, hard thrust. I grip her hips, too impatient to take it slow. Her muscles spasm around my cock, pushing me to the edge of an orgasm. I can feel her climbing with me, chasing another release.

"Oh God, Hunter! Yes! Harder!" I love the breathy rasp of her voice as she begs me for more. When I can't hold back anymore, I slide my hand between us, brushing my thumb over her clit. As soon as she spirals out of control, her pussy tightens around me, and I let myself crash over the edge with her. My orgasm pulses through me, so intense my legs begin to shake.

"Holy fuck! Faith... Jesus Christ." I steady my elbows on either side of her, sucking her nipple into my mouth, nipping, licking, and caressing as we bask in the afterglow of our shared release.

I can't even speak. I could stay here in this moment with my cock buried deep inside her forever. I'm bereft when I have to pull out, but I'm actually lightheaded. I slump down onto the bed, and Faith crawls under the covers, snuggling against my chest as our breaths calm, and we fall into a blissful, sated sleep of tangled limbs.

Chapter 4

FAITH

"EXACTLY HOW MANY times have you watched *National Lampoon's Christmas Vacation?*" Hunter's eyes are just about popping out of their sockets right now.

"It's my favorite holiday movie. Why?"

"Looks like you bought enough Christmas lights to illuminate the entire neighborhood. Maybe even the entire state." He's making fun of me now, but I don't care. I always vowed that when I had my own house, I'd have lights covering the roof.

"Would you begrudge your wife the chance to fulfill a childhood dream?" I bat my eyelids at him, hamming up my butter-wouldn't-melt smile.

"God, woman, how do you do that? If I could wrap someone around my finger like that, I'd rule the world."

"Aww, shucks, you say the sweetest things!" I continue unloading the decorations from the car.

"I guess I better call someone to come put all this up."

"What? No, we need to do it ourselves. That's part of the fun. We can rope Coop and Zee into helping us!" His furrowed brow tells me he's not exactly on board with this plan.

"No dice. One or both of us would break our necks. Have you

seen how high the roof is on this place? You can't walk in a straight line without incident. Do you really think I'd let you up a ladder with Christmas lights?" I don't have a leg to stand on. He makes a valid point.

"Okay, I'll concede on the outside décor. But we do all of the inside by ourselves. It won't be any fun if some interior designer comes in and decorates for us."

"By no fun, you mean they would make the house the epitome of elegant holiday décor?"

"All I heard there was, blah blah blah, bland Christmas."

"When did elegance become synonymous with bland?"

"The day you married me. Come on, Hunter, it will be so much fun. We can have trees in all the rooms, garlands round the fireplace, and twinkling lights everywhere. It'll look great. Trust me." My plea is falling on deaf ears. He thinks I'm going to create a Christmas decorator's nightmare, holiday décor Freddy Kruger would be proud of.

"Okay, Faith. I'm trusting you not to turn this place into a clown's Christmas fiesta." Part of me wants to make the place completely garish now that he's thrown down the gauntlet, but I don't want to ruin Christmas. This is our first holiday season, so I want it to be a time we both can enjoy.

"Now, can you help me unload the rest of this, Mr. Grinch? I'll reward you in the bedroom later."

"Well, I don't know about my heart growing three sizes, but I'm pretty sure I have an appendage that definitely just grew three sizes."

"Oh my God, I'll never be able to look at the Grinch the same way ever again. Dirty boy."

"You love it."

"I sure do!"

When we finish bringing everything inside, I search through the bags for the first Secret Santa item I purchased. It would be too easy and obvious if it were for Hunter, so I decided on a little something for Zee. I'm going to have it couriered to her right now. I'm hoping she assumes it's from Coop, but when she figures out it was me, she's going to pitch a fit. It's going to be hilarious.

We've been planning on having dinner with Coop and Zee this week. Just low-key at the house, and then maybe going out for drinks after. I've been ready and waiting for the past thirty minutes, giddy to see my best friend.

"What's your deal today? You have that look of mischief in your eyes, Faith. I can spot it a mile away."

"Nothing. Just happy we're going to spend some time with our friends." I let out a maniacal laugh, totally giving myself away. I have a terrible poker face. How am I going to pull off some Secret Santa antics on him if I can't keep this to myself?

"Spill."

"Okay, but promise you won't tell them. It's in the title, this is supposed to be 'secret.'" Before I get a chance to spill my guts, the doorbell rings. "They're here!"

"A word of advice, love… you need to calm down if you want them to have any mystery about whatever the heck you just gifted them." He follows me to the door, holding it shut with his hand for a moment. "It's all tactical. You have to assume they are telling each other, so they are coming here knowing that it's you or me. Take a deep breath and relax your face. You look like the cat that got the cream right now."

I do as he says, trying to shake out the giggle that's desperate to escape me. When I've taken a beat to compose myself, I open the door and am met with a very stern face from my best friend. I can see Coop is trying to keep his expression as blank as possible, but he's really struggling.

Hunter erupts with laughter as he takes in the sight before us.

Zee is dressed head to toe, cosplay, Santa's little helper. It looks even better than I anticipated. Never one to shy away from a dare, she's rocking cute little elf ears, candy cane stockings, a super sexy elf tutu-type dress, and even the hat with bells on the end—the whole nine yards.

With Hunter unable to contain his amusement, Cooper loses it, doubling over as he walks in the door.

"I hate all of you." Zee sounds *pissed!* She prods us all in the chest, hammering home her sentiments. "All. Of. You."

"Oh shit, we're going to be on the naughty list." She's shooting Hunter a venomous look right now. Coop can see she's not best pleased and tries to mitigate the tension.

"Babe, you should be thanking whichever one of these clowns gifted you this outfit. You look bangin'. Seriously, your breasts are so fucking hot in that bodice. I'd definitely risk getting coal in my stocking for a naughty night between the sheets. Will you keep it on for me tonight?" Zee tries to stifle a laugh, but she can't stay mad for long, mainly because I know she's already plotting revenge. She'll cover her bases and make sure we all get a gift as equally embarrassing, if not more so.

Reaching into her purse, she grabs something and hurls it at Coop. *It's coal!* I have to clamp my hand over my mouth. I'm actually whimpering. I'm trying so hard to contain my laughter, but the fact that she committed to the task and brought actual pieces of coal with her is hysterical.

She reaches for another and then another, hitting Hunter right in the fun-zone and catching me right in the boob.

"Ouch! Not the boobs, Zee." For some reason, that just makes the boys laugh even harder. It's not until I drop to my knees, laughing so hard I'm worried I'm going to pee myself, that I notice the shoes.

"We are *not* going out for drinks tonight, I hope you all know that." She taps her foot in consternation, but it draws Hunter's attention to her elf shoes as the jingle bells ring out with every tap.

"Fuck that, we're *definitely* going out to a bar. The rules of Secret Santa were clear. You have to roll with it. We had a plan for dinner here and drinks at a bar."

"I'm going to make you sorry for this, Vaughn. Just wait until the next social gathering. I'll have you sporting a Santa banana hammock!" When Coop can't stop laughing, she throws him under the bus too. "Maybe I'll get you boys a matching set. You think this is funny?"

"You're right, Zee. It's not funny. It's fucking priceless is what it is. I'd gladly wear a banana hammock to see you cutting a rug in the bar tonight." He gives me a sly wink, and I realize he's riling her on purpose, so I don't give myself away.

"I have to agree with him, babe. Heck, I'd go out buck-naked if it means seeing you in this getup. You're smoking hot, Zee." I can tell she's about to make Coop pay for that comment. Her eyes narrow the way they always do when she's hatching a plan.

"Then you won't mind all the attention I'm going to get. Sexy elf in a bar full of red-blooded men? They are going to be lining up to sit on my lap and tell me exactly what they want for Christmas." Resting her hands on her hips, she may as well shout checkmate.

Hunter ushers everyone to the kitchen, attempting to take the heat off his best friend. Cooper looks positively murderous at the thought of a bar full of men ogling his woman. I hold back, walking behind Zee because I can't stop smiling with every step she takes. Those little bells are priceless. I'm going to pay for this in our wager, but right now, it seems totally worth it.

Zee only picks at her dinner, but she seems in good spirits by the time we're ready to head out. If anything, my best friend has embraced the challenge and is full of Christmas cheer as we head out on the town.

Broadway is the place to be in Nashville—live music, great crowds, and an awesome atmosphere. The moment we step out of the car, our little party of four draws attention. That's become the norm for me now. Hunter is recognized everywhere we go, then throw in Coop, who's still playing for the Titans, and you get a media storm. Add the fact that I have my own hashtag on social media and add a sexy elf of a best friend. Tonight was never going to be a covert outing.

Titans' fans swarm us, asking for autographs, but the moment they set eyes on Zee, there's a shift in the crowd. Women keep shouting my husband's name, but their men only have eyes for Zee.

"I've been a good boy this year."

"I'm on the naughty list, sweetheart."

"My Christmas wish came early." Zee catches that last comment and makes a point of holding the offender's gaze.

"I'm sure that's not the only thing that comes early." Coop shrugs out of his jacket and drapes it over Zee's shoulders in an attempt to cover her up. He's a man on a mission, pushing his way through the crowd with Zee tight at his side. He's tackling like he would on the field, and Hunter is quick to follow Coop's path with his arm firmly around my waist.

When Coop secures a VIP area in one of our favorite bars, Zee hands him back his jacket, sporting a smug grin.

"Reap what you sow, champ." She waves at onlookers as she fluffs her dress to take a seat.

"I didn't come up with this 'gift.' It was one of those two fuck-nuts," he says with his eyes firmly on Hunter.

"Lighten up, Coop. Isn't that what you told me before we left my place? It's just a dress, right?"

"It's not the dress I'm worried about, it is every fucker in this place getting an eyeful of your tits and ass. They are practically salivating."

"Well, my tits and ass as you so eloquently put it... are mine. They aren't your property, so if I'm okay with a few stares, it shouldn't bother you, now should it?"

"Bullshit. I don't own you, but your body is most definitely for my eyes only."

"You didn't just say that." I feel bad that what I thought was a harmless prank has become divisive.

"Guys, don't let a harmless gift ruin your night. This is supposed to be fun, remember?" Coop rolls his eyes as he scans the room.

"I'll have fun giving each of these letches a harmless punch in the face. Fucking savages." Zee is a headstrong woman. Coop would do well to learn that fast if he wants her to stick around. Thankfully, she seems amused by his visceral reaction. She definitely seems smitten with him, no matter how much they bicker.

She opens her purse and holds it out to Coop. "Do you want

some of my coal to lob at them, baby?" She gives him such a sickly-sweet smile that he can't help but laugh, and just like that, our evening is back on track. He pulls her in for a passionate kiss, staking his claim.

"Get a room, guys." Coop ignores me, if anything, deepening their kiss to prove a point. *He's never going to back down when it comes to Zee.*

Hunter leans in, caressing my ear with his lips. "Come dance with me. Let's leave these two to suck face."

"Me? Dancing? Do you really think that's a good idea? I'm wearing heels, which skyrockets the probability of me falling on my face or stepping on your toes."

"I'll take my chances." He sweeps me up and onto the dance floor, his strong hands wrapped around my waist as we sway to the music.

"I've got to hand it to you, Faith, that was an inspired Secret Santa gift. Not sure Zee sees it that way."

I finally let myself fully enjoy it, letting out a giggle I've been holding for hours. "Epic, right? And the shoes… oh my God. When she was tapping her foot all angry and the bells were ringing, I almost peed a little."

"You realize you've set the tone now? This is going to be a contest of embarrassing each other relentlessly until Christmas."

"Maybe I'll earn myself another hashtag." He spins me around the dance floor before his lips crash down on mine.

"What am I going to do with you, Mrs. Vaughn?"

"Take me home and ravish me?" I pull him in, unwilling to relinquish his kiss. Butterflies take flight in my stomach as he deepens our kiss—or maybe it's sugar plum fairies. Everything else just falls away when I'm in his arms—the crowd, even the music. I lose myself in his caress and the delicious scent of his cologne. I can feel his cock straining in his pants, the hard length of him pressing into my hip. I could mount him right now and not even care that there would be a room full of onlookers.

"Easy there, tiger. Y'all are drawing more of a crowd than Zee." Coop always looks out for Hunter, but I resent it right now, or should I say, my libido resents it! "Maybe pick a less conspicuous spot to dry hump each other."

Hunter fists his hands in my hair, keeping me a whisker's breadth from his lips. "Duly noted, bro, but I need a minute. If I walk off the dance floor right now, my raging boner is going to be tomorrow's news headline." I know I shouldn't, but I find the whole public arousal thing seriously hot. He allows himself one last taste of my lips, his tongue caressing mine with a promise of what's to come when we get home.

My pulse is racing as Hunter struggles to compose himself, knowing that I don't have any hope of doing so myself. He's intoxicating. It's not until I hear jingle bells at my back that the spell is broken.

"Have I suffered enough yet? Can we bounce?"

"We've only been here for thirty minutes."

"Yeah. Thirty minutes too long. This place is full of leering, rabid horndogs. I think Coop is going to be carted out in handcuffs if we stay much longer." Hunter relinquishes his hold on me, leaving me bereft, heading over to talk to Coop.

"I thought you were all about making him jealous?"

"That's much more fun in theory than it is in practice. My elf tits are going to be trending on Instagram before the night is out. I've already clocked at least a dozen people snapshotting with their phones."

"You really do look smoking hot."

"I know. I'm freaking sexy, Christmas arm candy, but I don't like the fact that I want Coop to be jealous. I'm not that girl. You know me. Easy breezy." There's something in her gaze as she glances in his direction.

"Okay, girl. Let's get you and your wondrous, festive tatas out of here."

"I'm going to hate myself for this tomorrow, and I'll make you delete it, but we may as well take a selfie to document the beginning of the war."

"The war?"

"The Secret Santa war. You may have won your little sex wager with Hunter, but after my baptism of fire tonight, I'm going to be out for victory on this one."

"Heaven help us all."

"You know it!" I pull out my phone, holding it out and up as far as my arm will allow. Everyone knows you get the most flattering selfies that way. When I look at the picture, I can see the mischief in my best friend's eyes. She's concocting a plan of attack as we speak. This wager just got real—real sassy.

Chapter 5

HUNTER

FAITH HAS BEEN MAKING headlines again this week on *TMZ*. She and Zee have been gracing social media in snapshots from our elf night out. Coop's been too busy with practice and games to be too bothered by it.

There have been a few Secret Santa items floating between the four of us, but nothing too crazy right now. I'm not expecting it to last with our trip to Aspen looming. We leave tomorrow, and I'm preparing myself for the prospect of some pretty embarrassing pranks. Zee is definitely biding her time after the elf costume.

So far, I've stuck to the more traditional version of our little game. I've sent Faith some smoking hot lingerie that really was a gift for me. I sent a Christmas kissogram to Coop during practice the other day, which I heard about from all the other guys on the team. I'm told his face was quite the picture when a jolly old man in a red suit showed up to serenade and plant a bearded kiss on him. I'm ninety percent sure he knows that was from me.

Faith has been up to her usual hijinks but on festive steroids. I think she felt bad about the elf costume even though Zee was pretty good-natured about it after the initial embarrassment. She was laughing about it the next day. I asked Faith where she got the outfit because I really want to see my wife in a sexy elf getup. It doesn't need to be limited to an elf, she could be sexy Mrs. Claus—sexy anything really. As long as there are Christmas stockings involved and adorning her killer legs, I'll be a happy man.

"Hunter, there's a huge box out here with your name on it." Faith appears at the bathroom door, her gaze traveling the length of me, fresh out the shower and sporting some morning wood after contemplating her in stockings.

"Open it."

"Did you order something?"

"No." Shit. This is a Secret Santa delivery, I'm sure of it.

Faith disappears for a moment, returning with a huge package.

"Love, I'd have gotten that." She lays it down on our bed.

"It's not crazy heavy. Come on, open it."

"Is this one of your pranks?"

"This wasn't me."

"Damn. I was hoping it was. That means it's from Zee or Coop, and my money is on Zee."

"If it were Zee, the package would be much smaller. You don't need a box for a banana hammock. It would fit in an envelope just fine."

"Tell me she wouldn't do the speedo thing. I can't go out in public wearing nothing but a cock sock."

"How is it any different than her being out with her booty and baps on display?"

"Come on! That isn't a fair comparison. Plenty of women wear revealing dresses in a bar. If I went outside in a banana hammock, I'd be arrested. I don't make the rules."

"I'd bail you out."

"Just open the box, and let's get this over with. We've got a plane to catch in a few hours." She rips off the tape like a kid on Christmas morning. She bursts out laughing, and I'm not prepared for what she pulls out—it's a suitcase. There must be something in it. A suitcase isn't worthy of tears in my wife's eyes from laughing so hard.

"Holy crap!" She can't contain her amusement. "This is

straight-up amazing." Turning it around to face me, I see what has her in hysterics, but I'm not laughing.

"Fuck off. This has Coop written all over it. He's a twat. Not even Zee would inflict this on me. I'd gladly take the cock sock right about now."

"There's a note." She hands me an envelope.

"Great. Is it my last will and testament? I'm going to die of embarrassment. The paparazzi are going to have a field day with this."

"What does it say?"

"I don't think I want to know." I slide a piece of paper from the envelope, shaking my head because I can guess what this is going to say.

To Hunter, Santa says you've been a naughty boy this year, but he took pity on you and is giving you your Christmas wish. Be sure to pack your clothes in this suitcase, but first, remove the contents and make sure to carry them as hand luggage. Happy travels!

"What's inside? Unzip it." I'm glad my wife finds this so amusing. She knows fine well what's inside the case.

"I assume it's my brand-new penis pump to go with my personalized penis pump advertisement suitcase. How the fuck did he do this?" Somehow my asshat of a best friend has managed to get a picture of me that I recognize from a Gatorade ad a few years back. He's had it photoshopped. Where there was once a Gatorade tumbler, there's now a penis pump. If that wasn't bad enough, there is a banner across the top that says, 'I'm not ashamed to admit I need the *Penis Pump 2000* to turn my wiener into a winner!'

There's a website address along the bottom, which I'm praying to God isn't real.

"Here it is." Faith takes great pleasure in handing me my ridiculous looking penis-torture device. Fucking hell. It makes my cock hurt just looking at it.

"Grab your phone and look up this website, www.huntervaughn-hasatinydick.com. I swear to God if he's put dick pics on the internet, I'm going to shove him off a cliff in Aspen."

"There wouldn't be pictures of your manhood. It's massive. I can attest to that. He'd have to find teeny-weeny pics to put up there."

"Missing the point, Faith. It doesn't matter if it's my cock or not. People will assume it's mine."

"I doubt it. You get caught with a semi all the time when we're out in public getting a little too frisky."

"Will you just check the damn URL?"

"Don't get testy. Get it? Testy!" When she sees the absolute lack of amusement on my face, she quickly searches on her phone. The way she throws her hand up over her mouth to hold in a guffaw, I have my answer.

"I'm going to kill him!"

"It's not a big deal. It's kind of funny. Admit it. If you had thought of this, you would have one hundred percent done it to Coop." I pace the floor, running my hands through my still-damp hair.

"Of course, I would, but that's not the point. You know this is going to be all over social media the second we set foot in the airport."

"A wager is a wager. You can't break the rules."

"We broke the rules of our little wager multiple times. Why do we have to be sticklers for them now?"

"Because... just because. It's funny. We can brainstorm something really good to get him back."

"Isn't that a violation of the rules? We're not supposed to team up. Every man for himself and all that."

"We're married. I declare we have been joined as one in the eyes of God, and this wager is linked to the celebration of his birth, so we can totally team up without telling Coop and Zee."

"You're a devious little minx."

"And you love me for it."

"Fuck, yeah, I do."

"We still have time before we have to go to the airport. Care to show me that massive trouser snake of yours before we leave?" She doesn't have to ask me twice. I drop my towel, relishing the way her breath catches when her eyes fall to my rock-hard erection.

"Open your legs, Faith."

I can't believe I have to walk through the airport with this ludicrous bag and a fucking pump in my hand. How am I going to explain this at check-in? The second the driver pulls my bag from the trunk, I can hear the people around us begin to whisper and snigger as my awesome new suitcase comes into view. The driver manages to keep a straight face, so I reward him with a huge tip.

People are fumbling for their phones, desperate to snap a picture of my current humiliation. Faith attempts to mitigate the situation, but her uncanny ability to put her foot in it shines through.

"What a funny gift," she says in an exaggerated tone, her voice loud enough to draw attention. She sounds like a bad infomercial. "If there's anyone who does *not* need a penis pump, it's you. Your cock is huge even when it's flaccid."

Holy Fuck! Did she just use the word *flaccid* in the same sentence as my cock? If I thought the pump in my hand was bad, this is exponentially worse.

"Please stop talking."

"What? I'm helping. Here, I'll swap you my suitcase for the pump." She moves to grab it, but I guess she's expecting more resistance. She yanks it out of my hand, smacking herself in the face with it.

Onlookers are doubling over, laughing at the slapstick routine playing out in front of their eyes. Great. Faith is going to have a black eye from a fucking cock pump. Can this day get any better?

Why do I even think these things? It's like I'm goading the fates. Faith stumbles back, her eyes closed after taking that hit. I let go of my suitcase and reach out to grab her before she trips head over heels on the corner of her case. I manage to catch her just in time, but her flailing arms and subsequent swing of the pump jabs right into my Adam's apple.

I find myself gasping for breath, having had the wind knocked right out of me.

"Oh God, Hunter, are you okay?" I can't answer her when it feels like I've had my windpipe crushed by a Louisville Slugger. Someone eventually comes to our aid, but the second I set eyes on him, I want to kick him in the nuts—Coop.

"Well, fuck me. We're not even there yet, and y'all are getting into mischief." Coop helps Faith steady herself, leaving me to piss in the wind. I'm going to ram that pump up his ass for this.

Zee starts shooing the crowd that has gathered around us.

"Get out of here. Haven't you ever seen a penis pump and a grade-A klutz before? Go about your business, people." As they begin to disperse, I catch a glimpse of Faith's eye—it's swollen and already starting to bruise. I cough a few times, finally finding a sharp intake of breath.

"Love, are you okay? Jesus, your eye."

"I'm okay. I didn't mean to throat punch you with that thing. I'm so sorry."

"I don't care about me, I'm worried about you." She wraps her arm around my waist, staring up at me with one eye shut.

"Argh, maties! I can be a Christmas pirate." Zee chuckles at her best friend's odd sense of humor.

"You can sail the seven seas. The great Captain Candy Cane on the good ship Wankster."

Coop looks just as bewildered as me watching the girls descend into a fit of giggles.

"Chicks are weird." His brow furrows as he stares at Zee.

"Ours are weird. I'm not sure the rest of womankind can be held accountable for their particular brand of crazy."

"True."

Then he sees my suitcase, and his laughter echoes through the airport foyer.

"I'm about to sucker-punch you, Coop."

"Totally worth it, bro. That thing is priceless! Seriously genius."

"Yeah, yeah. Laugh it up."

"I can't believe you're actually using that suitcase. There's no way in hell I would. Some things are more sacred than a wager, a handshake, and a man's word. Defending my manhood trumps everything else."

"Maybe I'm just more secure about my cock measurements than you." I pick the pump up off the ground and hand it to him. "You can have this if you want. I've seen you in the showers after practice, and you could use the help." He lobs it at the nearest trashcan.

"Why were you staring at my junk in the showers? I never realized you felt that way about me, bro. Sorry, I just don't find you physically attractive."

"I seriously need you to stop right now. I just got slugged by a fucking penis pump, and my wife will have a shiner in the morning."

"Boo-freaking-hoo. You didn't have to watch every guy in Nashville ogling your girlfriend in an outfit that was strictly for the bedroom."

"Let's just get out of here." Between the two of us, Coop and I grab all the bags and suitcases while the girls amuse themselves. Faith doesn't even seem fazed by her swollen eye. I suppose her pain tolerance has probably grown over the years, along with her clumsy limbs. The minute we set foot on the plane, I'll have them bring an icepack for her. Depending on how it looks when we get to the ski lodge, I can call in a doctor to take a look at it. At least for now, she seems happy.

I've never been so happy to check a suitcase in my life. Navigating the first-class lounge is easier without a giant cock pump advertisement. Lucky for me, Coop threw the actual device in the trash, so I'm spared that humiliation from this point on.

The flight goes by quickly, and I half-consider not grabbing my bag from the carousel, but then my picture holding the fucking pump would be going around and around for everyone to see. It seemed the lesser of two evils just to pick up the damn thing and make like a tree. I'll be buying a new suitcase for the flight home.

When we arrive at our lodge, my earlier embarrassment is long forgotten. I switch my phone off to avoid seeing any social media frenzy surrounding the debacle at the airport. It can wait. The snow-capped mountains are breathtaking, and this lodge is amazing. All the home comforts you could want while on vacation with an awesome view of the ski slopes.

After putting our bags in the bedroom, Faith slips into something more comfortable—an oversized Gryffindor sweatshirt and yoga pants. Not exactly what I had in mind, but damn, she looks hot in anything. Laying back on the bed, I watch as she moves around the room, throwing her hair up in a messy bun and removing her contacts in favor of glasses. It looked sore when she had to get the contact out of her swollen eye, taking at least five attempts to remove it. Even with a black eye, she's every bit the sexy librarian when she wears her glasses.

She turns to see me eyeing her with a greedy stare.

"Have you been using that pump?"

"What?"

"I can see you're rocking a tripod right now, or is that a third leg I've never noticed before?"

"Why don't you hop on and find out?"

She climbs onto the bed, crawling up until she can straddle me, grinding against my cock through the fabric of my jeans. Faith turns me into a horny teenager every time she does something like this. I'd take a dry hump from her any day of the week and thank her for it.

As she leans down to kiss me, I see her eye up close.

"Jesus, Faith, your eye is so swollen. Maybe we should go to the hospital to get you checked out."

"I can see fine, I haven't detached my retina or anything. It's a bruise. I'm not going to explain to a doctor that I socked myself in the eye with a penis enlarger. Do you want to explain that one?"

"Not particularly, but I'd whip my cock out if it meant making sure you're okay." She ghosts a kiss on my lips accompanied by a torturous grind of her hips.

"Then whip it out, big boy. I guarantee it will make me feel better."

That's all the encouragement I need.

Coop and Zee will have to wait for dinner. I'm hungry for something else entirely at this moment. If this is any indication of our trip, it's going to be a vacation to remember. Snow, sex, and skiing. A perfect combination. I just hope Faith survives the rest of the trip unscathed.

Chapter 6
FAITH

SKIING ISN'T my strong suit. I doubt I'd need to point that out to anyone who has ever met me, but it's worth repeating after two days of lessons and zero vertical wins. Hunter was right when he decided that skiing wasn't something he could just walk me through a few times, and I'd get the hang of it. In fact, I'm not sure why he thought this would be a good vacation activity for me. I'm glad we're here because, despite my inability to balance in any way, I love it.

The snow is the epitome of holiday vibes, and the lodge we're staying in is awesome. Even just sitting by the fire and looking out over the snow-capped slopes is totally worth the trip. My only complaint would be the lack of a Christmas tree and twinkling lights. I'm not mentioning it to Hunter because I know he'd immediately set about getting this place decked out with every decoration known to man. He's already gone out of his way to make this special, and I love it.

I get the impression that this trip was originally planned as a getaway meant for two, although I'm so happy to be sharing the experience with Coop and Zee. Having my best friend around makes any situation enjoyable. Seeing her and Coop interact for an extended time is a little strange. There's something not quite jiving between them, but I can't put my finger on it.

We've had a few Secret Santa items delivered while we've been here, and I'm almost certain that they are Hunter's doing. Nothing embarrassing or crass, but genuinely sweet, thoughtful gifts. He doesn't really let other people see his softer side, but I know it well, and I'd put money on these gifts being from him. He gets to gift without owning it. Heartfelt, thought-out presents for each of us without admitting he put so much effort into picking out items he knew we would like.

Hunter isn't shy about showing his affection for me. He'd never hold back. But when it comes to Coop, I see him holding back at times. Heaven forbid he comes across as less than one hundred percent alpha male. Coop is like a brother to him. They played together for years with the Titans, and with Hunter being the veteran of the team, Hunter became Coop's role model. Their friendship just grew from there, and to look at them now, you wouldn't think there's an age difference. It's the same with Hunter and me. Okay, it's clear that I'm younger, but if you met Hunter on the street, you would think he was in his late twenties. He's in peak physical condition, hot as Hades, and his personality is younger than his years.

From the moment I sat down with Hunter in that hotel bar at the beginning of the summer, I didn't see age—not mine and not his. As corny as it sounds, we are kindred spirits and made for each other.

When I come down for breakfast on the last morning of our trip, there's a box sitting on the kitchen counter with my name on it. Thinking it's another sweet gift from Hunter, I rip it open, excited to see what he sent. God, this is going to be an interesting one. He's letting his wicked side come out to play.

There's a note attached to the box.

If you want to stay on Santa's good list, it's time to get a little naughty. Put the remote back in the box.

You'll find an envelope in your purse with instructions on when and where to use this gift. Most importantly, don't tell anyone about this. Enjoy! Secret Santa

Holy Toledo, Batman! This is going to be one heck of a day. I quickly go in search of my purse, anxious to know when I need to use this ridiculous gift. I'm not worried. There's no way something like this even works. It's going to be a cakewalk.

I go about my day, sipping hot cocoa by the fire and looking out at the snow. The world exists under a blanket of snow, making every peak and valley seem magical. We are cocooned inside the lodge, the perfect way to relax and unwind.

Hunter and Coop have gone skiing every day, but after a disastrous lesson, my instructor begged me not to take to the slopes. I'm not sure that's ever happened before. When I told Hunter, he couldn't contain his amusement, and I could see he was relieved to hear it. He's been fussing over my black eye, trying to convince me to go and get it looked at.

I'm so glad Zee is here. She's a wizard with makeup and helped me cover my embarrassing bruise almost completely, so I didn't draw attention. I could just imagine the headlines if Hunter Vaughn's wife is seen sporting a black eye. Then, I'd have to explain that *#LadyFumble* strikes again.

As it's our last night here, I wanted to set up a little surprise for the rest of our group, but there's been a change of plan. What was going to be an intimate dinner for the four of us and a magical sleigh ride through the snow, is now an obligatory ball at the lodge. Me in heels and a fancy dress and all eyes on Hunter. It's a recipe for disaster.

Zee stayed with me today, letting the boys go and enjoy some bromance time on the slopes. She's pretty good on skis, but she seems a little under the weather. Not ill, but just not herself. I still can't put my finger on it.

"So, how are things with you and Coop? You've been together for a while now." I hand her a fresh cup of hot cocoa with ten marshmallows, just the way she likes it. I settle down at her side and pull the blanket over our legs.

"We don't all fall head over heels like you do. Literally and figuratively."

"So, you don't love him?"

"We've been casually dating for less than five months."

"That's only a few months less than Hunter and I. And I don't think you could call our first few months together dating. Maybe loosely."

"You and Hunter are the unicorn of relationships. Your situation is very different to Coop and me."

"In what way?"

"How much time have you got?" Her tone is a little snarky.

"Plenty, so fess up."

"Well, let's start with the most obvious difference. You were a virgin on a mission. You got together over a wager. You have that adorable clumsy charm that men find endearing. Everything about you two has been at warp speed, and I'm not saying that's a bad thing. It's just not the norm. You're lucky. You both are."

"You and Coop aren't exactly moving in slow motion. You jumped into bed with him the night you met, and for the most part you've seemed pretty tight since then."

Zee shifts uncomfortably next to me.

"Are you slut-shaming me right now? You wagered your virginity."

"Wow! Really? When have I ever shamed you for anything? Throwing my virginity at me is a low blow."

"I'm sorry. You hit a nerve, that's all. I didn't mean to be a bitch. Forgive me?"

"Yeah, but I might Secret Santa your ass with something humiliating."

"I've had enough humiliation. Whoever is sending the gifts on this trip has my vote for being the winner. Awesome, thoughtful presents. I wasn't expecting that." I'm about to tell her about the package I received earlier today, but then I remember that the note said not to.

"Can I ask you a question?"

"Does it matter if I say yes or no? You'll ask me anyway."

"You don't seem yourself lately. Is everything okay? Are you not happy with Coop?"

"I don't know. It's weird because you're married to his best friend. If we stop seeing each other, then I'm not going to see you as much."

"You're my best friend, Zee. You're going to be a part of my life no matter what. Dating Coop for the sake of easy social gatherings isn't a reason to stay with him."

"I guess."

"If you're not feeling what's written all over his face, then you shouldn't let it drag on. It wouldn't be fair to either of you." She leans her head on my shoulder, letting out a long sign.

"I think maybe you're reading too much into his face, bud."

"He's crazy about you. Anyone can see that."

"Can we not talk about this? I just want to enjoy our last day here, looking at the snow falling and hanging with my bestie." I wrap my arm around her shoulder, eager to comfort her.

"I'll shut up for now, but when we get home, you and I are having a proper talk about this. Okay?"

"Sure." As if on cue, the boys arrive back from skiing, their cheeks red, and when Hunter comes over to plant a kiss on me, his skin is freezing cold.

"Hey, love. Do you want me to put the water on for a bath? You must be chilled to the bone after all this time."

"Only if you're going to join me."

"Barf!" Zee fakes shoving her fingers down her throat.

"Sounds like a good idea. You want to join me in a bath, Zee?" I don't care what Zee says—Coop is hook, line, and sinker for her.

"Why not? We need to start getting ready for dinner, anyway." Coop's brow furrows ever so slightly.

"Don't do me any favors, Zee. Fucking hell, you'd think I just asked you to put your neck on a chopping block."

I take Hunter's hand and pull him away from the car crash we're witnessing right now. It's best to let them argue without an audience. When we get to our room and close the door firmly behind us, Hunter is quick to prod me for details.

"What the hell was that all about? Are they having problems?"

"I can't betray Zee's confidence. She's my best friend." I head into the bathroom, desperate to say no more on the subject. This could get messy if we stick our noses where they're not wanted.

"And Coop is my best friend. He has a right to know if there's something going on."

"You're right. I'm not disputing that. But it's not our place to meddle. They have to find their own way, and I don't want it coming in between us. If it doesn't work out, they'll still have to see each other when it comes to us. They won't be able to put it behind them and just move on."

"Is that what's going on? Zee doesn't want to be with him? I thought they were getting along. Sure, they bicker, but lots of couples do." I turn the faucet and let the hot water drown us out for a few moments.

"They need to work this out themselves. We just have to be supportive friends."

"Okay."

All thoughts of our best friends fade into the background as Hunter strips out of his ski gear, standing naked before me as I run my hand back and forth through the bubbles.

"See something you like, Mrs. Vaughn?" It's a rhetorical question. He knows I want him. It's written in the lines of my face, in the way I bite down on my lips as my gaze rakes over the length of him —greedy and unabashed.

"I have no idea what you're talking about." I can't contain the smile creeping in at the corner of my lips.

"Then, why are you licking your lips like you're ready to eat a cock pop?"

I like to tease him, knowing it's all a game. We know exactly where this is going to go.

"Is that those things you get at Starbucks?"

Amusement dances in his eyes as he slides his hand down his abs before reaching for his cock.

"This isn't available in a coffee shop, love." A thrill runs through me, my pulse racing as my breath quickens. I scramble to switch off the faucet while my eyes remain firmly on Hunter.

"I... I..." He has a self-satisfied expression as my brain short-circuits, lost in a haze of desire.

"Cat got your tongue, Faith?"

"No. Cock's got my tongue." I pull my sweater up and over my head, dropping it to the floor before quickly pushing my pants over my hips and kicking them off.

I step into the bath, settling in with my arms over the side of the rolltop tub, gesturing for him to come closer. He steps toward me with an easy grace, but the tightly corded muscles of his shoulders betray him. His gaze is fixed on my lips.

"You've got a wicked little mouth on you."

"Then put it to good use." He moves away from me, stepping into the tub to sit opposite me. "Why aren't my lips wrapped around your cock right now?" I'm somewhat surprised. It's not often that Hunter would turn down the chance at a good blow job.

"Plenty of time, love. For now, I just want to soak in the tub with you and enjoy the way your breasts look when they are covered in bubbles. Pretty damn hot." I cup my breasts, teasing him as I flick my fingers over my nipples.

"They do feel good when they're hot and wet, ready and waiting for you." He puts his hand to his mouth, biting his knuckles.

"Holy shit, my wife is hot."

"You're not so bad yourself, Vaughn. But why are you all the way over there on the other side of the tub when you could be inside me?"

"Because I'm trying to be a good friend, and so I need you to tell me what's going on with Zoey. Is Coop about to get dumped?"

"I told you, I'm not going to betray Zee's trust. It's unfair of you to ask me. Please don't push me on this because I love you, and I want to share everything with you, but when it comes to their relationship, I think we need to take a step back."

His hands stroke up and down my calves, the soft lap of the displaced water a soothing balm between us.

"I'm sorry, love. I'm just worried about Coop. He really didn't seem like himself today, and Zee has been hot and cold with him this whole trip. I'm just trying to have his back. I won't ask you again."

Sliding his hand further up my legs, he pulls me toward him, water sloshing over the side of the tub.

"Mr. Vaughn, we need to get ready." He thrusts two fingers inside me, hitting just the right spot to spark a fire of desire deep in my core.

"We have enough time for this." He drops his head, his lips sliding over my nipples as he thrusts a third finger inside of me. I give myself over to his kiss and the pleasure his touch brings to every nerve ending in my body.

Fisting my hands in his hair, I pour all of my desire and desperate need for him into this one kiss, losing myself when he withdraws his fingers and positions his cock at my entrance. He slams into me, making me take every last inch until I'm seated to the hilt. Then, he lets me set the pace, riding him as hard and fast as I dare. He looks glorious beneath me, his toned abs disappearing between the water's surface to where our bodies meet.

There's something about the way he leans back, spreading his arms out over the rolltop tub. His hair is dripping wet, rivulets of water running down his face, falling to his lips as he bites back a growl of satisfaction. He lets his head fall back, giving me complete control of his body and his pleasure.

"Fuck, Faith." My name is a whisper on his lips—a melody—a song of worship to the way our bodies come together in perfect harmony.

The faster I buck my hips, the more I lose control, climbing higher and higher until I can't hold back any longer.

"Hunter, I'm so close. Oh God! Oh God!" The moment the words leave my lips, he wraps his arms around my waist, holding me steady as he takes over, setting a punishing rhythm. As I crash over the edge, he chases his own release, shouting my name as he dives into a spiral of sensation with me. Every fiber of my being is consumed by this man.

We ride out the aftershocks in each other's arms, the water long gone cold.

I'd love to crawl into bed and get lost in Hunter for the night, but we have a dinner dance to go to. Hunter always gets roped into making public appearances no matter where he goes. Vacation is no different. I know he'd have turned it down, but this is an altogether unorthodox request.

As fate would have it, Hunter's mom is in Aspen with her new beau. We only have one night of overlap, but she insisted he bring me to meet them. He says that she's only interested in showing him off to her vapid ski buddies. So, we're going to the equivalent of a snow- engulfed country club. Apparently, they have a winter ball every year, so it's dinner, cocktails, and dancing.

Hunter's mom didn't come to our wedding. She had some cruise booked well in advance and insisted she couldn't cancel. He offered to pay any rescheduling costs, but she wouldn't hear of it. I understand his reticence to be paraded around like a prized bull. In truth, everything she has is because of her son. He takes care of her every need and whim. I'm more than a little nervous to meet my new mother-in-law. I'm sure she read about us in the papers, and *#Lady-Fumble* is a whole other reason for me to be concerned.

When we finally pull the plug on the tub and set about getting dressed for the evening, it dawns on me—my Secret Santa gift. I'm supposed to wear it tonight.

Shit, shit, shit!

Chapter 7
HUNTER

I COULD THINK of five things I'd rather be doing tonight. Shoving a hot poker in my eye makes it onto the list. My mom is a formidable woman now that she has my money to fund her every want and need. I don't even want to think of the millions of dollars she has wasted on frivolous, useless crap. I never realized how materialistic she is until money became of no concern.

It's hard to be a vapid, materialistic shrew when you don't have two dimes to rub together. That was the story of my childhood. She worked two jobs to keep the crappy roof over our heads, but the second I made it big, her personality changed. I'm her red rosette pony to trot out whenever the mood strikes her. There's a reason I haven't introduced her to Faith yet, and it has nothing to do with Faith.

My mother is going to look down her nose at Faith because of everything she's read in the media. I know her. She doesn't wait for the facts or give anyone the benefit of the doubt. I guarantee she's already made her mind up about my wife. If I had known she was going to be here, I'd have booked a vacation for literally anywhere else on the planet.

The saving grace of tonight is that Coop came along on this

trip. My mother loves him, and he can handle her embarrassingly shameless flirting. I'm not sure Zoey will be too thrilled, but I'm going to need her to suck it up for one night. Coop is going to be Faith's human shield. I don't even need to mention it to him. The second he hears my mom is in town, he gives me a look that tells me we're on the same page.

When we arrive at the venue, it's all flashy cars and valets scrambling for tips. I had gowns and suits delivered to our lodge today as this shindig is black tie. Funnily enough, I didn't anticipate going to some stuffy charity ball while we were on vacation, so alas, I didn't pack a tuxedo in my penis pump suitcase. *Fuck.* I can just imagine the tongue lashing I'm going to get for 'embarrassing her' with my antics.

Faith looks stunning tonight in a silver ballgown—perfect for a winter princess. Her hair cascades down her back in a waterfall of soft waves. I can't take my eyes off of her as she steps out of the car. She gives me a sly wink when I look down and catch a glimpse of her shoes—she's wearing a pair of Tiffany blue Chucks.

"Wise choice, love. I'd rather we not end up at the hospital. I plan to sweep you across the dance floor tonight in this dress. You look incredible. Like Cinderella."

"Good luck getting close enough to me to dance. There are about four thousand layers of tule in this thing."

"You don't like it? You should've told me. I'd have gotten something else delivered." She reaches out to take my hand as we head inside.

"I love it. Stop worrying." I'm not completely convinced as her tone seems a little reticent.

"You seem on edge. Are you okay?"

"Just nervous about meeting your mom. What if she doesn't like me?"

"Faith, I don't want you concerning yourself with anything my mother has to say. She's an insipid hypocrite. Let's just get through the small talk and then enjoy the rest of our night. There's food, alcohol, dancing, and our friends are with us." Faith's gaze travels to our friends, who seem deep in conversation as we find our way to the ballroom.

"They seem happy, right?"

"I'm not sure, but they definitely sounded happy before we left the lodge. Your friend screams like a banshee when she comes. How did you ever sleep when you were roommates?"

"She wasn't in a constant state of orgasm. And the answer is earplugs, really good-quality earplugs."

"I feel weird that I know what your best friend sounds like when she comes. We need separate lodgings next time."

"Why?" she says with mischief in her eyes. "Did it turn you on?"

"No. I don't see your friend that way." I'm flustered to say the least. I didn't expect her to ask me that.

"I know, but it was kind of hot hearing them. It felt kind of naughty to overhear such a passionate outcry, don't you think?" Is this a trap? Is she trying to trip me up here? My only defense is offense.

"Did it make you wet, love?" I pull her into my arms, my lips mere almost touching hers. "You like hearing your friend screaming in ecstasy?" Her breath catches, the rise and fall of her chest quickening, her breasts heaving against the hard lines of my torso.

"I…"

"Tell me, Faith. Say it."

"Yes. It turned me on."

"Why?" I guide her onto the dance floor, leaving Coop and Zee to find our table. "I want to know what was going through your mind, Faith. What were you thinking when you heard her come?" God, Faith's body is coiled and ready, craving my touch.

"I thought about how beautiful she must look, naked and lost to the throes of passion. How full and perfect her breasts must be."

"Keep going," I whisper in her ear. I'm struggling to compose myself as she writhes more than she sways to the music.

"I wondered what she tastes like. If she's sweet like honey… if she tastes like me."

"Jesus, Faith." I wanted to get her a little hot under the collar, but this—her fantasy—is so much hotter than I could've imagined. "Would you taste her, Faith?"

She nestles her head against my chest, shyly avoiding the question. It would never happen in real life, and I know she's just saying all this to get a rise out of me—literally a rise out of my cock—but part of me wants to know how her fantasy plays out.

"Maybe." Her voice is small, a breathy whisper. I lift her chin, forcing her to look into my eyes.

"You don't need to be shy with me, Faith. You're my wife, and whatever you fantasize, I want to know."

"Is it weird, though?"

"No. If you wanted to act on it, I'd have a problem. I won't share you with anyone, male or female. But if something turns you on, then I want to hear it. Talk dirty to me, love."

"Not here. Not in a room full of people."

"Then, I guess I'll have to find us a quiet corner at some point this evening."

A voice cuts through the music, requesting that everyone take their seats to welcome the benefactor of this evening. Faith makes a move toward where Coop and Zee are already seated, but I stop her in her tracks, leaning in so only she can hear.

"You didn't answer the question." I wrap my arms around her from behind, pulling her against me, letting her feel how much she's turning me on right now. "Would you taste her?"

"Yes." It escapes her in a hushed confession, a fantasy that will never be realized. I wouldn't let anyone touch Faith, not even her best friend. It doesn't stop my cock from becoming hard as a rock at the idea of her being turned on by a woman.

As we take our seats, my wife is blushing, and I know she's pressing her thighs together under all those layers of dress. She's wet for me, and right now, there's nothing I can do to alleviate the ache for either of us.

"What's up with you?" Zee looks to Faith with a sly grin. She's up to something.

"I'm fine. Just hot in this dress. I think there's more material in this thing than everything in my closet put together."

"I hear you. I'm about to burst out of this. My breasts look freaking amazing in this dress. Look at them. Bangin', right?"

Faith doesn't speak, her body jolting slightly before she slams her hands down on the table, drawing attention from the other people at our table.

"Oh God!" There was a sultry tone to her voice. I had no idea she was this turned on. She looks like she's about to climax if Zee mentions her breasts again.

"Are you okay, love?" I slink my arm around her waist, pulling her and her chair close to my side.

"I'm fine. I just…" She thinks better about whatever she was about to say, her brow furrowed as she grips the edge of the table.

"Are you sick?"

"No!" Her breath is ragged as she busies herself smoothing out the abundant layers of her dress.

"Okay. No need to snap at me. You just seem out of sorts. This isn't about what we were just talking about, is it? I was just kidding around with you. It was harmless."

"I know, I know… oh God, yes… I know. *Stop!*"

"Stop what?"

She looks across the table at Coop and Zee. "I don't know. Just stop." They both look bewildered, but I have a feeling one of them is faking it. This has Secret Santa written all over it.

"Faith, what the heck is going on?"

"I can't tell you. I thought it was from you. By the look on your… face…" She stops for a moment, biting down on her lip, her eyes shut tight. "It wasn't you."

I'm about to lay into Coop and Zee for whatever they have done to her, but I'm interrupted by an unwelcome voice behind me.

"Hunter, darling, I'm so glad you're here." I stand from my seat to greet her.

"Hello, Mother." She's giving me air kisses like a fucking moron elitist. I can't even begin to convey my distaste for her fake niceties.

"Cooper!" She leaves me hanging, brushing past Faith to get to her beloved Coop. "You look simply edible as usual. It's not fair that you keep getting more handsome, and I keep getting older."

Coop flips the switch and gives her a winning smile. "Georgia. You look ravishing as always. I don't believe that you've aged a single day since the last time I saw you." It makes me cringe to see my mom pawing at him, throwing her head back with an insipid laugh. Zee looks as pissed off as I feel.

I guess it's now or never.

"Mom, I'd like you to meet my wife, Faith."

Faith stands from the table but quickly grabs hold of the edge, almost doubling over. I can't tell if she's in pain or—fuck—she sounds the way she does when I'm about to get her off. My mom eyes her with disdain.

"Hell-*wow*, Mrs. Vaughn. Please excuse me for a moment. I need to use the restroom. *Oh!*" Her body jerks, and she accidentally pulls the tablecloth, sending cutlery, drinks, and the centerpiece crashing to the floor. My mom looks horrified, but Faith attempts to recover her introduction. "I'm so happy to finally meet you. Hunter has told me all about you."

"All terrible, I'm sure." She reluctantly accepts Faith's proffered handshake.

"Not at all." My mom knows it's a lie. We don't exactly hide our dislike of each other. I love her—she's my mother—but loving family doesn't necessarily come with an obligation to like them. My mom and I definitely fall into that category.

"Sweet of you to lie, dear. I see your hashtags do, in fact, do you justice." She looks around at the carnage all over the floor. Hundreds of dollars in booze alone, spilled down the front of Faith's dress.

"Gosh, I'm so sorry."

I wrap my arms around her, pulling her close to my side as if I can somehow shield her from my mother's judgment, not that I give a shit what my mom thinks of Faith and me. I know it will mean something to Faith. She wants people to be accepting of us, especially after what happened with her folks.

"Don't worry about it, love. The waiters are already on their way to clean this up and reset the table. It's no big deal. And I can have another dress here for you in twenty minutes. Do you want the same one?"

"Sure. I'm just going to go to the restroom to get the worst off of this and hide in shame."

"It could happen to anyone." I can't keep a straight face as I try to reassure her. She knows as well as I do that no one is more prone to fumbling mayhem than her. There's a reason for that. Anyone clumsier than her hasn't survived to adulthood. She's like those people who make the record books for the most ridiculous way to die in freak accidents, and yet she's still living and breathing.

"Liar. But I l-o-o-ove you!" Her breath is short and sharp as she clings to my arms. If my hands were elsewhere on her body right now, I'd think she was having... *holy shit!*

"Faith, are you... tell me that you're not doing what I think you're doing right now in a room full of people." She pulls me into her arms, her nails digging into my back as her body begins to shake. She bites down on her lip and lets a low moan escape her.

"Hunter. Secret Santa." She can barely get the words out as my mom stands in gaping horror. "Underwear." Jesus Christ, her nails scratch my neck as she struggles to keep any kind of decorum in this moment. "Vibrating. Get the remote."

Holy fuck. She's about to have an orgasm in front of a room full of people. I'm going to kill whichever one of them bought this. Her pleasure is mine. It isn't for anyone else to see or influence with a fucking remote.

I lean in and whisper in Faith's ear. "Fake fainting. I'll catch you." Without hesitation, she gives an Oscar-winning performance, allowing me to sweep her up into my arms and make a fuss about taking her to a private room to give her a few minutes to check she's okay. Before I leave the table, I turn to Coop and Zee, my distaste evident in the furrow of my brow and the low growl aimed in their direction.

"Hand it over. Whichever one of you fools has the remote, shut it the fuck off." They both drop their gaze to the floor. "Where is it?" Neither of them look up. They are in on this together. I can't fault them for that because Faith and I have done the same thing, but I'm really pissed off right now. My wife is writhing in my arms, still being bombarded with the vibrations coursing through her body.

"Hunter. Get me out of here, now. I can't hold off much longer."

"I've got you, love."

"I'm going to be back here in an hour, and you jokers better watch out." They are stifling their laughter—not at Faith—at me. They can laugh it up, but stealing an orgasm from my wife is going to cost them in this wager.

I follow the waiter to a private room with Faith cradled in my arms, my mom muttering something about me being a colossal embarrassment, but I really don't give a fuck right now.

When the door closes behind us, I set her down and lock the door.

"Did I hear you right, you're wearing vibrating underwear?"

"Yes. Oh God, it's doing it again. Holy crap." She stumbles over to a couch, trying to quell the overwhelming sensation. She can't even get to the underwear through all the layers of her dress.

"Lay back, love. I'll get them off, and then I'm getting *you* off." I unbutton my tux jacket and shrug out of it. It's too constricting to be able to forage through the tulle. I drop to my knees in front of her, reaching for layer after layer of her dress, trying to find her legs. I'm cursing my dress choice for her in this moment. How could she even stand to be in this? It's like a fucking sauna wading through all this material.

Faith whimpers as her underwear continues to vibrate. God, I'm hard as a rock hearing her moan. I pull off my bowtie and loosen the top button of my shirt. When I finally catch hold of her left leg, I follow the trail, my hand caressing her calf and up the inside of her thigh. I can hear the buzzing noise, but as my fingers trace a line over to the sides of her underwear—lace—I get distracted by how fucking hot my wife looks in this scrap of vibrating lace.

"Oh God, Hunter… I have to come! Oh fuck!" I'm not about to leave her unsatisfied. Instead of divesting her of the offending panties, I pull them to the side, just enough to thrust two fingers inside her. She's fucking soaked, her arousal intoxicating my senses as I push the mini vibrator against her clit.

"Let go, Faith. I've got you." I set a punishing rhythm with my fingers, my cock aching to be inside her. She detonates, so much pent-up frustration trying to hold back.

"Oh my God! Yes... Hunter... oh God... yes!"

"That's it, Faith. Let me hear you, love." She's lost in wave after wave of orgasm, her muscles tightening around my fingers, making my cock twitch in my pants. I need to be inside her. As she rides her release, I pull my fingers from the warmth of her sex just long enough to unzip my pants and position myself at her entrance. With a hard thrust, I sink balls deep, and she feels so fucking good— warm, wet, and tight as a drum.

As I circle my hips, I grab the sides of her underwear and literally tear them off. I can still hear the vibrator as the panties fall to the floor. I can't even see Faith's face right now with a mountain of dress between us. Her voice is muffled, but I can just make out what she's saying.

"Move the dress. I can't breathe with it all shoved in my face." Without thinking, I just grab layers of tule and start ripping them as I continue to grind my hips. I couldn't pull out right now, even if I wanted to. My cock is begging for relief.

"Rip the layers, Faith! Fuck, I can't pull out. You feel too fucking good. Do you want me to stop?" My brain is screaming, *please don't ask me to stop!*

"No! Don't stop. Please, God, don't stop." I continue to thrust, her hips moving in time with my own as we tear at the layers of fabric until we meet in the middle. She immediately fists her hands in my hair and pulls me in for a kiss, her lips crashing down on mine in a desperate plea for more.

I feel like I'm having sex in a candy floss machine. Fucking hell, I'm never buying Faith a dress of this magnitude ever again. This is making it almost impossible to have hot, dangerous sex in a public place—*almost*. Designers really need to think of this shit. I want to touch my wife's body right now more than I want my next breath, but literally, the only spot I can reach is with my cock. Lucky I'm well-endowed, or this might have been an impossible feat.

"Hold the ripped shit out of the way, love. I need to grab your hips, and I can't fucking see them." Faith starts laughing, which would make any man flaccid, but I know my girl. This is just par for the course.

"I'm trying." I slow my pace to help her, but she just yells at me through a mound of silver tulle. "Don't stop! I'm so close, please, Hunter, don't stop!"

"Then grab the damn dress." She yanks it out the way and up into her face. Now all I see is her sweet pussy. Fuck, if I wasn't ready to come before now, I sure as hell am now."

"Come with me, Faith. Say the word, and I'm yours." I press down on her hips, holding her steady, and I hammer into her, letting her take every last inch of me as deep is she can handle.

"Now, Hunter. Oh God, I'm coming." Her muscles start to spasm, her thighs trembling as she screams my name. I lose control, chasing my own release as she rides wave after wave of ecstasy. A string of expletive, unintelligible words pour from my lips, and I come, my cock pulsing inside of her.

It takes me a few minutes until I can make a coherent sentence.

"Holy shit. You're so fucking hot when you come, even when you're stuck in the center of a marshmallow."

"Does that make you the smore? Give me smore, Hunter, smore!" She amuses herself with that one, a little snort giggle escaping her.

"I'll be the smore for your soft, warm center any day of the week. Anytime, anywhere."

I reluctantly pull out, still sporting a semi. When I look at Faith, realization damns—her dress is in tatters, she has no underwear, and the minute she stands up, she'll have my cum trickling down the inside of her thighs. How the fuck are we going to get out of here?

Chapter 8

FAITH

HUNTER'S FACE is painting a grave picture right now. Not what I'm used to right after he orgasms.

"What's wrong?"

He wrestles his cock back into his pants before running his hands through his hair the way he does when he's stressed.

"Look at your dress." I look down, and I must not be seeing whatever is making him purse his lips and furrow his brow. Sure, it's ruined, but it was already ruined with half a bottle of red wine from the table I so gracefully destroyed.

"I'm sorry. Was it really expensive? It was such a beautiful dress."

"I don't care about the dress, Faith." I'm distracted by the buzzing viber panties on the floor.

"Is it the panties? I thought they were from you. Obviously not by your reaction at the table."

"No, it wasn't me, and it's not that. How am I going to get you out of here without drawing the attention of the five hundred or so guests who are mingling outside that door? You're in a torn dress, and you're full of my cum right now. Where's that going to go when you have no panties. I don't relish the idea of my spunk marking the hotel carpet like a snail trail."

I can't contain myself. I laugh so hard I'm more worried about peeing myself than of Hunter's cum spilling out of me.

"Oh my God, that's hilarious!" He stares at me, dumbfounded.

"How are you so calm right now?"

"Come on! Get it? *Cum* on. It's not the end of the world." I can't stop laughing. "The visual on that is hysterical. I can just see it now. Me walking out with handfuls of my dress and leaving a trail of cum in my wake. I can just imagine the hashtags now. Lady Cum-ble. Fumble Cum-ble. Lady Jizz. Vulgar Vaughn. Oh, can we make that one *Vulva Vaugh*? It doesn't really tie in with the jizz theme, but I like it."

I finally get a laugh out of him. Mission accomplished.

"Where do you come up with this stuff? We're *not* adding any hashtags to your catalog, especially not ones that are related to my spunk. Any other woman would be freaking out right now, but you're already making fun of yourself. This, right here, is why I fucking love you."

"Because I don't mind being caught in public with no underwear and your man juice running down my leg?" I love the sound of his laugh. It speaks to my heart on a molecular level.

"Please don't ever call it man juice again."

"What about man milk?" He throws his head back with a full belly laugh, making music to my ears.

"That's worse!"

"Baby batter? Cock snot? Penis Colada? Yes, I like that. If we walk out and anyone asks, I'll just tell them I had a few drinks. Slinging back the Penis Colada."

"I'm going to piss myself if you don't stop. Holy shit, woman. You have the dirtiest mind, and you come out with stuff that would shock the locker room."

"Why thank you, kind sir. For your praise, I'll enjoy your snake spray all the more as it slithers down my inseam."

"Seriously. We need a plan. This is all shits and giggles, but how am I getting you out of here and into a car?"

"Call Zee. Ask her to go to the gift shop and buy me an outfit. There has to be a gift shop in this joint. Get her to bring some baby wipes as well." His eyes light up, and he stalks over to me, planting a mind-altering kiss on my lips.

"You're a fucking genius."

"It was the cock snot that sealed it, right?"

"I love you, Faith Vaughn. Life will never be boring with you around."

"Damn straight."

With my superior intelligence agreed on, Hunter pulls his phone out of his pocket and dials Zee's number.

"I need you to find the gift shop and buy your bestie an outfit. We're in the private conference room down the hall to the left of where you're at right now." I can hear her asking him why she needs to buy an outfit for a wine-stained dress. I stifle a chuckle. She's going to die when she sees the state I'm in.

I grab the phone and speak to her, woman to woman.

"Zee, I look well and truly fucked right now. Literally. Corset ripping, jizz-tastic. I'll be arrested if I walk out into the ballroom. Can you just go and get me some pants and a shirt already? And get me some wipes. I'm a sex-mussed mess." Hunter puts his head in his hands, and I'm not sure if he's laughing or horrified—or both.

When I hang up the phone and hand it back to him, the look in his eyes tells me he's definitely amused *and* horrified in equal measure.

"Is there nothing sacred, woman? Did you really have to divulge all that to her?"

"What do you think would happen? You've met Zee. There's no chance that she'd let this slide. Hell, there's a fifty-fifty chance that she provided me with vibrating underwear tonight. I think that says everything you need to know about the lack of boundaries between her and me."

"It better have been her. If Coop was responsible for this and was using a remote to give you an orgasm, I'll rip his nuts off and feed them to him."

"It was Zee. I'm certain of it." I'm not really sure, but Hunter looks like he's about to pop a vein in his forehead at the slightest possibility.

I start talking about Christmas gifts I've ordered for everyone we know, attempting to distract him until Zee gets here with something for me to wear. I don't even want to think about how Hunter's mom is going to react when I reappear in a different outfit and sex hair.

Maybe we can avoid her altogether. I'm already the worst daughter-in-law on the planet, so I may as well sidestep that landmine on my way out.

When there's a knock at the door, I jump to my feet, forgetting that I'm not wearing any jizz-catching undies.

"Shit."

"What happened?"

"Cock snot, snail trail." Hunter is trying so hard not to laugh at me right now, but I can see the smile creeping in at the corners of his mouth.

"Sit down and wait until I check that it's Zee out there and not some random stranger about to witness what looks like the set of a porno gone wrong."

I do as he asks, mostly because I'm not overly fond of the feeling of liquid dripping down my leg. Hunter opens the door a few inches, thinking he can grab the clothes and shut her out. It's almost as if he's never met my best friend before. If there's an opportunity to mock me, she's going to take it.

Zee can be pretty strong when she wants to be. It's as if she turns into She Hulk. Pushing the door, she muscles through the smallest gap, and her face tells me everything I need to know about how I must look right now.

"Holy Mother of God. You weren't kidding when you said you're well and truly fucked." She turns and winks at Hunter. "Good work, big boy. Color me impressed."

"Can you just give her the clothes already?" Hunter looks mortified as he picks up his jacket, buttons his shirt, and puts his bowtie back on. If only it were that easy for me to put myself back together.

Zee hands me a bag, and when I pull out the sweatshirt she

bought me, I'm less than enthused. It has a giant *Rocky and Bullwinkle* on the front. If I thought I was getting out of here without drawing attention, this is the death nail in the coffin.

"What the hell?" She smiles at me with her butter-wouldn't-melt face.

"They didn't have a plain shirt?"

"No. It's a fucking gift shop, Faith. It's not exactly couture. Now the pants on the other hand, I just couldn't resist." *Great.* I pull the pants out of the bag, and it's clear that God hates me. Why in the hell would a gift shop want to sell pants with a million tiny Santas on them?

"These are pajamas, Zee."

"It's all they had. It was either that or an adult onesie with the button back flap. I figured this was safer. Knowing you, the flap would open, and you would bear your chocolate starfish to the entire ballroom. Trust me, this is the less-offensive option."

"Fine. Thanks. I'll be out in a few minutes."

"I'm assuming you won't be hanging around for the rest of the evening?"

"You think? And here I was thinking I'll fit right in!"

"Don't get grumpy. Should I call a cab to take us back to the lodge?"

"Yes, and tell Coop to make apologies to my mom, so we can avoid her abject horror."

"Done." She disappears out of the door which Hunter promptly locks to let me change. He has to wrestle me out of the corset so I can slip out of what's left of my dress.

"Nice." He stands back and admires me with a heated stare as I stand naked before him. "Do we have time for round two?"

"You can get round two when we're back at the lodge. I just want to get out of here and avoid your mother seeing me like this." I quickly pull on the ridiculous Santa pajama bottoms and my Bullwinkle sweatshirt. When I'm good to go, Hunter grabs my hand, pulling me into his arms.

"You're still unbelievably sexy, even when you're wearing the craziest outfit. Are you ready? We're going to get a few stares on our way out. We need to be quick. No tripping over your own feet, okay?"

"I'll do my best. I don't exactly plan these things."

The coast is clear as we head out into the hallway. Maybe we can sneak out without encountering a barrage of onlookers. It would be nice to have at least one of my mishaps go unnoticed. Coop and Zee have arranged a car at the back entrance. There's only one door we need to get past without incident, and then we're golden.

I literally creep down the hallway, much to Hunter's delight.

"You can walk normally, you know. When I said we need to be incognito, I didn't mean you had to skulk around corners like a jewel thief."

"That would be exciting. I could see myself as a jewel thief."

"Oh really? You think you could break into a vault and live in the shadows? The very fact that we're tiptoeing down a hallway right now speaks volumes."

"Okay, so maybe I couldn't be a cat burglar."

"More like an elephant... with a megaphone... on roller skates." I'd be annoyed by that comment if it weren't so completely and utterly accurate.

When I think we're home free, one of the doors to the ballroom swings open. As always, I have impeccable timing. Out of hundreds of revelers, I manage to lock eyes with Mrs. Vaughn. Fuck me. Her facial expression is one of abject horror as she eyes me from head to toe. I'm happy I haven't seen myself in a mirror as yet.

"Hunter!" Her voice echoes through the room, drawing all eyes to where she directed her banshee call—us.

"Shit, shit, shit." The color drains from Hunter's face as he stands frozen to the spot, pinned by his mother's beady gaze.

"Keep moving, Faith. You're about to get photographed by all and sundry if you don't haul ass."

"What about you?"

"I'll distract my mom and the rest of the vultures. I'll meet you back at the lodge. Coop and Zee are waiting for you." I steal a quick kiss before leaving Hunter to fend for himself. I feel like Cinderella running out on the grand ball, except I'm not a princess in the making. I'm the pumpkin!

"Love you, babe. Sorry!" He slaps me on the behind as I take off at a sprint. It's a risky move because I may well fall flat on my face. I'm really happy with my shoe choice tonight. Chucks are my new favorite sneaker. If I were wearing heels right now—forget about a quick getaway.

When I throw open the back exit, Coop is holding the car door open for me. It's like something out of a movie and totally lends itself to my earlier jewel-thief idea of hopping into the getaway car to outrun the cops. In my scenario, my new mother-in-law is the cop. I'm sure I have made a lasting impression.

"Where's Hunter?"

"He said to go without him." Coop jumps in and slams the door shut as he barks out the address. It's only when the hotel is a speck in the rearview mirror that I turn my attention to Coop and Zee.

"Which one of you fools sent the panties?"

"It's supposed to be Secret Santa. You can't ask us as per your own rules." Is she really quoting my hair-brained wager at me right now?

"Well, I'm just letting you know, it better have been you, Zee. Hunter is pissed that a room full of people almost saw me having an orgasm. If he thinks for even a second that your boy here was responsible…"

"What the fuck?" Coop interjects.

"Remember how you felt in the bar when guys were looking at Zee's tatas?"

"Don't remind me."

"Well, imagine that those guys were getting to hear her moaning and writhing in front of the aforementioned horny guys." His brow furrows at the mere thought of it.

"Point taken."

"I'm more concerned about the fact that Hunter's mom hates me. It's not likely that she didn't already have a low opinion of me after everything she must have seen in the press. I had one chance to make a good first impression in person, and that just went up in smoke. I'm going to go out on a limb and say she won't be joining us for the holidays."

"I wouldn't sweat it, Faith. She's always been a bit of a shrew. There's no love lost between her and Hunter. He won't give it a second thought. He'll placate her tonight, and by tomorrow morning, it will be of no concern to him. I promise."

"I hope so." I appreciate Coop trying to make me feel better, but I can't help feeling like I've let Hunter down.

Zee wraps her arm around me, squeezing me to her side.

"So viber panties… they actually work?" She gives me a sly wink and instantly lifts my mood.

"Oh my God. Seriously, I might have to buy another pair. So hot. If it were under different circumstances, I'd be down for letting Hunter loose with a remote for my panties."

"What happened to the ones you were wearing?"

"Hunter ripped them off."

"Okay, when we get back to the lodge and Coop isn't listening, I want details."

Coop feigns being wounded. "Why don't I get to hear?"

"Because you're a horndog. This is girl talk, and unless you've grown a vagina in the past five minutes, you don't fall into that category."

"I'm getting you a pair of those panties, Zee. I like the idea of having a remote for your panties." He wiggles his eyebrows at her, making her giggle.

"No dice, champ. I wouldn't trust you with the remote."

"Why not? You trust me to get you across the finish line in every other way I can think of."

"We aren't talking about this right now."

I still need answers. Tonight has been a colossal clusterfuck, but I can see the funny side of it. After all, I started this wager with Zee's elf costume. I set the tone, and it came back to bite me in the ass, or should I say vibed me in the vagina?

"What happened to the remote?"

"I don't know." Coop and Zee speak in unison. One of them is lying right now, and when I find out which one of them was pressing the buttons, I'm going to enjoy exacting a deliciously dirty revenge.

When we arrive back at the lodge, all I want to do is crawl into the tub and wash off my makeup, the wine I managed to cover myself in when I wrecked the table, and my sticky thighs. Dried semen isn't the nicest feeling in the world.

Pulling up outside the lodge, I'm relieved to be back in our own quiet space. I wish Hunter didn't have to stay behind. I'm sure I'll hear all about the carnage when he gets back. For now, I'm going to enjoy a very long soak in the tub.

Zee still looks absolutely breathtaking, not a hair out of place. She managed to get through the evening without wrecking a dress, getting caught with vibing underwear, and having super loud sex in the hotel. The last part was worth every moment of embarrassment. When Hunter gets lost in the moment, he becomes so dominating, primal, and desperate for the release that only I can give him. It's a heady feeling—intoxicating and empowering.

As soon as I set foot in the door, I leave Coop and Zee to whatever they've got going on and disappear into my room. The tub is every bit as enticing as I imagined on the way home. My muscles ache from orgasm after orgasm. I didn't realize how tightly I was coiled until now. The water is so hot, it reddens my skin, but it's also incredibly soothing. I lie back, letting the bubbles wash away tonight's grime.

After a while, I reach for my phone and pull up the *Amazon* app. I'm ordering some more of those viber panties. No matter what shenanigans went down tonight, I can't deny that the vibrating underwear was h-o-t! I ordered some for Zee as a Christmas stocking stuffer! She'll definitely get a kick out of them.

I let myself wander down the *Amazon* rabbit hole finding and ordering all kinds of weird and wonderful little inexpensive gifts for Hunter and our friends. My finger hovers over the one-click button on a specific gift set. Coop has gotten away with only cool gifts thus far. He hasn't endured the same comical humiliation the rest of us have dealt with over the past few weeks. We're running out of time to drag him down to our level!

The moment I hit 'buy now', I feel a pang of guilt, but it's short-lived. Hunter is going to find this hilarious, and that trumps anything else.

It's late when he gets back, but I want to hear what happened with his mom. He looks exhausted as he drops down on the bed beside me.

"Hey, love." He pulls me against his side. "You smell good."

"I soaked in the tub for a while when I got home. Do you want me to run you a bath?"

"No. I'll grab a quick shower. I'm too tired, and I just want to get some shuteye before we have to go home tomorrow." He sounds a little defeated, giving me cause for concern.

"How did it go with your mom?"

"It wasn't surprising."

"She hates me, doesn't she?" My heart sinks as silence spans between us. His lack of response gives me my answer. "I guess I shouldn't be surprised. I'm not the girl who makes a good first impression."

Hunter lets out a huge sigh before smoothing down my hair and pressing a kiss to my head.

"You made a good impression on me."

"Only because you got an eyeful of my breast."

"Don't be so hard on yourself, Faith. You're amazing, and I love you more than life itself. Anyone who doesn't see that isn't worth knowing. Besides, it wasn't you that my mom had a problem with."

"What?" He stares up at the ceiling, his gaze a million miles away.

"She thinks I corrupted you. How could you love a guy that's older than you? I've humiliated her with our antics in the press. She's ashamed to call herself my mother. Basically, she gave me all the love and affection I'm used to from her. Of course, she waited to tell me how disappointed she is until after I did countless photo ops for her and was paraded around like her little show pony." That just makes me mad.

"How dare she say those things. You're the most amazing man I've ever met, and you being a little older than me has never been an issue or a hurdle for me to overcome. I see you for who you are, and I love the strong, confident, successful, and kind man you are. I'm the lucky one. Being your wife is a privilege, and as for your age… you could pass for thirty without hesitation. You're smoking hot, in great shape, and I won't have anyone, including you, talk smack about my husband!"

"Thanks, love. I appreciate it. I'm going to go grab that shower, and I'll be back in a few minutes. It's been a long day."

Normally, I'd join Hunter in the shower, but he seems like he could use the peace and quiet. Instead, I stupidly check my social media accounts. Of course, there are pictures of me looking like Christmas threw up on me with unmistakable sex-mussed hair. I'm disappointed that they didn't get imaginative with the hashtags. I have a good mind to repost the pictures with some of my witty tags.

When Hunter reappears with a towel around his waist and water droplets dripping down his abs, I completely forget what I'm doing.

"Faith, you're drooling." He gives me a panty-melting smile, and all is right in the world.

"Can you blame me? I'm never going to tire of seeing you wet and in a towel."

"Glad to hear it. What are you up to?" He nods his head toward my phone. "Tell me you're not on social media. I'm sure there are already pictures of my mom that look like she's chewing a bee."

"I haven't seen them yet. There are, however, some stellar shots of me creeping to the back entrance in my super flattering pajama outfit."

"Love, why do you bother looking? It never ends well."

"I'm fine. It's funny, but their hashtags are unimaginative at best."

"Shut off the phone. Can we just live in our own little bubble for a few hours? It's exhausting having your every move documented and scrutinized." He seems battle weary. I know just how to cheer him up.

I pull up my latest order on *Amazon* and hold it out for him to see.

"I was thinking about our wager. Zee got the elf costume. You got the penis pump. I got the vibrating panties. The only person who hasn't been royally humiliated yet is Coop."

"When did this go from being Secret Santa to Secret Pranks?"

"I knew all those sweet gifts were from you!"

"Well, then, it's not very secret, is it?" I pull him down onto the bed, my lips finding his in a reverent kiss.

"I love you, Hunter Vaughn. You're a big softy."

"Don't tell anyone. That's our little secret." He winks and rewards me with a heart-stopping chuckle. "So, let me see what you have planned for poor Coop."

I turn my phone screen to show him my earlier purchase.

"I was thinking we could send it to him for the Titans' Christmas Eve party."

Hunter erupts with laughter.

"Holy fuck! Forget what I said about embarrassment, this is going to be hysterical. Coop is going to shit a brick."

Chapter 9

HUNTER

CHRISTMAS EVE HASN'T HELD much excitement for me since I was a kid. Now Faith and I are about to celebrate our first Christmas together, and I feel the magic of the season for the first time in twenty years—at least.

Tonight is the big Titans' Christmas party, and Faith looks breathtaking. After the last party we attended, I made sure she's wearing something more Faith proof. I've gone to this party every year for a decade, and it always felt like a chore. Seeing the guys on the team with their significant others and their kids, it always felt like a night to remind me of everything I didn't have. Money and fame can only get you so far in life. It doesn't bring love or family.

When I step into the room with Faith on my arm, I'm filled with pride. My life has changed so much since this time last year. It still seems surreal at times. I can look at Faith across a crowded room or in the comfort of our own home, and it hits me like a Mack truck— I'm the luckiest son of a bitch on the planet. It astounds me that we've only been together for six months. So much has happened in such a short space of time. Our relationship has been on warp speed since the beginning.

Faith came stumbling into my life—literally—and I was caught hook, line, and sinker from the moment I saw her in that hotel lobby bar. It wasn't the easy choice for us to be together, and we've faced our fair share of hurdles this year, but looking at her now, I can't imagine this ending any other way.

Every day is a school day with Faith. I learn something new about her with every passing day. She really has shown her kinky side during this wager. I shouldn't be surprised—we got together on a wager for her virginity. That, in and of itself, speaks to her willingness to color outside the lines. I'm still shocked at how devious her mind can be.

What she has in store for Coop is definitely walking a fine line. It will be funny as fuck, but he's going to be so pissed, and her timing is impeccable. He'd probably find it more amusing if it weren't a night with all of our teammates—his teammates. I still feel like one of the team, but I guess I'm not technically a Titan anymore.

I'm thrilled to be here catching up with the guys I played, partied, and traveled with all over the states for years. It has taken some getting used to, not being around them day in and day out. I even miss training with Coop and his constant jibes that I'm an old man.

Tonight is going to go one of three ways. I half expect one of two scenarios—either he'll flat out refuse to play tonight's game, or he won't bring it up at all. However, you can never rule out a third option with Coop. He might come in, all guns blazing, announcing it to the whole room.

Faith squeals when she sees Zee across the room, leaving me for dust to go and hug on her as if she hasn't seen her in months. Yesterday was clearly too long ago. Coop follows the trail back to me, and from the look on his face, he's pretty uncomfortable right now, and I'm his prime suspect. Why does everyone think I'm the perpetrator?

He attempts to storm over to me, but he's stopped in his tracks. I'm guessing Faith's gift set is causing some problems.

"What the fuck, bro? What have I ever done to deserve this shit?"

"Did it cross your mind that I may not be the offending wager participant here?" He's making me uncomfortable just looking at him twitching and adjusting.

"There's no way one of the girls would do this to me. Zee knows better. She's fucking laughing it up right now, soaking in every moment of my discomfort."

"You mean you're actually using it? One item or both?" I try to stifle my laughter, but his face is a picture right now. I just gave away that I know what the gift was, but I'd rather take the heat off Faith, at least for now. We're supposed to reveal who gifted what to whom at the end of the night. It might be a better idea to wait until tomorrow—let Coop simmer down a little.

"I don't renege on a wager."

"You're a better man than me, bro. There's no way I'd have gone through with it." He keeps shifting like he has ants in his pants.

Faith and Zee make their way over to us, giggling as they watch Coop moving every three seconds. Zee slaps him on the ass before planting a kiss on his cheek.

"Fuck! Don't do that, Zee. It's not funny. Every muscle twitch is hurting me right now." Faith tries hard to school her features, but she's failing miserably.

"Which one of you fuckers sent me a butt plug and nipple clamps?"

"Secret Santa," we all chime in unison.

"Faith's not the only one who lost her virginity in a wager this year. My asshole has been violated in a way that will fucking traumatize me for life. Do you have any idea how sore this shit is?" His word choice isn't helping the girls' attempts to stop laughing.

"I'd think it's impossible to shit right now." I should've kept quiet, but he lined that joke up perfectly.

"Are you seriously wearing nipple clamps right now?"

"Why else would I have a sweater on? You could see them through my shirt. Not only are my nipples fucking killing me, and my asshole will never be the same again, but I'm going to pass out at some point with heat exhaustion. If that happens, one of you needs to hide the clamps and the plug before the paramedics cart me off."

"I think you've got the plug pretty well hidden, Coop." Zee has zero sympathy for him right now. She's having way too much fun watching him squirm.

"Bro, you know I've always got your back, and I'd maybe stash the clamps for you, but you're on your own with the plug."

"How the hell am I supposed to sit down for dinner? I had to perch on my side the entire cab ride here, and don't even get me started on how bad it feels when you go over a speed bump with this crap."

"It can't be that bad," Faith interjects—wrong thing to say.

"I'm living a *Fifty Shades of Grey* nightmare, and I don't even get to be the dude. I'm the sappy girl who had no idea what the fuck she was getting herself into. We're supposed to be celebrating the birth of our Lord, and I'm over here with a metal thumb up my ass. The fact that it has a pink jewel on the end of it just adds insult to injury. Literal injury!"

I feel bad for him. He'll see the funny side of it in a week or two, but right now, he's miserable.

"Why don't you just go take it off? Take it out? I'm not sure what the right lingo is in this instance."

"Both. Clamps off, plug out." The fact that he's correcting me makes it even funnier.

"Seriously, which one of you sent them?" He stares each one of us down, looking for the slightest hint of an answer.

"We're not going to crack, so stop eyeballing us." Zee wraps her arms around his waist, but the brush of her body against his must have nudged the clamps.

"Ouch! Nobody touch me. I'm going to be in agony tomorrow, thanks to you chumps."

"Stop being such a baby about it. I showed my tits to half of Nashville, Hunter became a walking advertisement for dudes with tiny dicks, and Faith had a room full of people, including her monster-in-law, witness her joygasm."

"I'd take any one of those 'gifts' over having metal rammed up my ass!" Even he starts to laugh hearing himself bitch about it. The more he laughs, the more he flinches. "Don't make me laugh, it's chaffing my nips. Why the fuck does anyone *want* to use this crap?"

"You wouldn't think twice about suggesting this stuff to me. I bet you'd love tightening some titty clamps on my breasts, reveling in how I'd writhe beneath you as you tugged on the chain." Zee has a point. Just hearing her describe it makes me want to buy some for Faith.

"That's different," Coop protests.

"Why? Because I'm a woman?" I'm standing here willing my best friend to keep his mouth shut. There's no good answer to her question. We live in a world full of double standards.

"Fine. I'm a huge hypocrite. Yes, I'd get off seeing your blush pink nipples clamped. I would worship your tight little ass if I saw you sporting a plug. Sue me. I'm a red-blooded male, but at least I admit my double standards."

Faith is uneasy with where this conversation is going. Coop and Zee seem like they are on the verge of an argument, and none of us want that. Not tonight—not at all.

"It was me. I'm the Secret Santa offender. I call timeout. Go to the bathroom and de-plug yourself, and for God's sake, take the clamps off. I can't watch you twitching all night long." Coop is dumbfounded, his expression mirroring his girlfriend's in this moment.

"Faith? You're supposed to be the sweet, slightly more innocent one of us. You're a dirty little minx." Coop's demeanor instantly lightens. "Not going to lie, feeling a little better about it now."

"Leave it, bro. You don't want to finish that thought." I know where he's about to go, and it grinds my gears before the words leave his lips.

"What? Knowing it wasn't you makes me feel exponentially better. It's kind of hot that your kinky wife is the reason I've dipped my toe in the shallow end of the BDSM pool."

"A plug won't be the only thing rammed up your ass if you don't shut up." I know I shouldn't let him wind me up, but he's really pushing my buttons right now.

"Is this what y'all are into?" He turns his attention to Faith. "Did you buy him a matching set?"

"Don't ruin the surprise, Coop. His set is wrapped and under the tree. No pink for him, though. I got him a black one. And Zee? She's getting the size up from yours, but I added the vibrating option on hers. I went all-in for me. I'll be serving dinner tomorrow in my own sexy elf outfit, with the clamps and my Christmas-themed, red-jeweled super-sized butt plug. I thought we all needed a new tradition for the holidays." Zee is laughing her ass off, but it's short-lived.

"Really, Faith? I don't think your proclivities are appropriate party conversation." *Shit!* There should be some sort of world record for consistently putting your foot in it. Coach is standing right behind his daughter with a disapproving furrow to his brow.

"Dad. I didn't see you."

"Clearly." There's nothing I can say right now that makes this any better. Coop steps in and takes the hit.

"Coach. Great to see you. Sorry about that. Your daughter's proclivities are just fine. She was just pointing out that my actions tonight are wildly inappropriate. We all know I'm a horndog. It's a problem. I thought it was acceptable to come to the party sporting some of my… accessories. Faith was just calling me out on it. Looking out for her friend." Coach isn't buying it.

"You don't have to defend her, Cooper. I'm aware that my daughter doesn't seem to care if the world knows what goes on in her bedroom." I can ignore a lot of things, but the way he talks about my wife isn't one of them.

"Hold up. That's completely unfair. You walk in on a private joke and make all kinds of assumptions. I thought we were past this, but I guess not." Faith interlaces her fingers with mine, standing firm at my side even though I can see that she's fighting back tears.

"I'm not lying, Coach. Look." Coop throws himself on the grenade, lifting his shirt to reveal a rather painful-looking set of nipple clamps.

Faith and Zee start laughing, much to her dad's dismay. In their defense, it's pretty hilarious to see the shock and horror on Coach's face right now. Coop is a fucking legend.

As we draw attention, I'm anticipating my best friend realizing that he's giving the entire team a show right now. In true Coop style, he turns the tables and makes himself larger than life.

"That's right, guys and gals, I'm rocking the bondage tonight. I'll literally do anything to make my girl smile." He looks to Zee, and she's got a goofy grin on her face. I swear I don't know what's going on with them from one minute to the next. They are either loved-up or embroiled in verbal sparring matches with each other. In this moment, they seem to be the former.

The team is having a great laugh at Coop's expense, and it has the desired effect. Coach backs off, leaving us to our bizarre group dynamic. I reach over and tug on the clamps, pulling them off.

"Holy shit! What the hell, bro? That was agony." Coop doubles over, rubbing at his nipples, half laughing, half crying.

"You know you love it."

"You're a dick, Vaughn. I want to slap you for that, but I also want to hug you for getting that medieval shit off my chest. Is it wrong that my junk is tingling? Is that supposed to happen?" Only Coop could pull something like this off and come out the other side with everyone laughing *with* him rather than *at* him. If he could bottle that shit, he'd be able to take over the world.

When the crowd dissipates, and everyone goes back to drinking, chatting, eating, and dancing, I pull Coop to one side while the girls go to the restroom together. I don't really get why they go in pairs, but I'm happy to get a moment to talk to him without Faith.

"Bro, you went above and beyond tonight. I really appreciate you taking the heat off Faith. Things with Coach are… complicated. You didn't have to open yourself up to team ridicule, but I just want you to know that it meant a lot to me that you stood up for her."

"We're family. That's what family does, right?"

"Right." He pulls me in for a hug, slapping me on the back, a little harder than normal.

"You owe me for this shit. I better be getting something epic for Christmas from y'all."

"Isn't the butt plug gift enough?"

"Fuck off. The only reason I'm not going straight to the

restroom to take it out is because I'm scared I am literally going to shit myself. How long do we need to stay at this shindig?"

"I think you've been a good-enough sport. When the girls get back, we can head out. Are you guys going back to your place or Zee's?" His face sobers, and I seem to have inadvertently hit a nerve.

"I think we're going to my place. She's been a bit cagey about the whole thing. Our only firm plan is coming to hang with y'all for dinner tomorrow."

"What? Is everything okay with you two?"

"Of course. We've only been dating a few months. It's still pretty casual. Not all of us find someone and get married right away. You and Faith are something special. You're a lucky fucker, you know that, right?"

"I really do." As the words leave my lips, I see my wife across the room, laughing and joking as she and Zee weave their way back to us. Coop's right. I'm a lucky son of a bitch. Faith is all I never knew I wanted until she walked into my life.

It takes us a while to navigate our way out the door. Holiday greetings and goodbyes are always long when it comes to the Titans. We're a family—everyone on the team and their families. I'd forgotten that over the past six months. Coach was always a huge part of why I thought I belonged here. Now I see that it's so much bigger than just one person. Everyone in this room has impacted my life in some way, and each and every teammate helped shape me into the man I am today. Every moment, every milestone I celebrated with the guys on this team led me to Faith. For that, I'll always be grateful and proud to be a Titan.

Coop and Zee head off in the same cab, so I assume they are going to spend what's left of Christmas Eve together. I think when it comes to those two, Faith and I are going to have to take a step back and let them figure it out on their own. I just hope it doesn't get too messy.

Faith cuddles into my side in the back seat of the cab, watching as snow begins to fall, dusting the trees with a touch of Christmas magic. By the time we get to our place, she's sound asleep, and I don't have the heart to wake her.

Lifting her from the car, I cradle her in my arms—my sleeping beauty. She's out for the count. She rouses long enough to shrug out of her dress, and I slip her into the ridiculously cheesy pajamas she bought for us—matching Christmas onesies. I can't believe she convinced me to do it. She'd be none the wiser if I waited until morning to put mine on, but I'm a sentimental schmuck when it comes to her, and I want everything to be perfect.

Once she's tucked in bed, I set about getting the living room prepared for the morning. The Christmas tree lights bathe our home in a warm hue. I know it's corny, but I fill Faith's stocking on the fireplace and spend an hour wrapping her gifts before placing them under the tree.

Before I crawl into bed, I reluctantly change into my onesie, knowing it will make my girl happy when she wakes up next to me on Christmas morning.

Chapter 10
FAITH

"MERRY CHRISTMAS!"

I can't believe he wore it. It's six o'clock, but I'm wide awake and full of the excitement that comes with Christmas morning. I never really lost the joy and anticipation of Christmas. Waking up next to my husband just makes it even more special, and the fact that he's wearing the matching PJs I bought is the cutest thing ever.

"What time is it?" Hunter's voice is so sexy in the morning, all low and gravelly.

"Six."

"Love, go back to sleep."

"I can't. I'm too excited."

"Just five more minutes. Maybe ten. I only came to bed a few hours ago."

"Okay." I kiss him and wait a few minutes until I know he's fallen back to sleep. I'm going to make him breakfast. I always make cinnamon rolls on Christmas morning. I used to take some to the neighbors growing up, and I thought it might be nice to keep that tradition going. I'll make a few batches and deliver them to our neighbors. I use the title loosely because this house has so much land around it, I'll have to hop in the car to get to each of the neighbors on either side of us.

I take my time, listening to Christmas songs and singing along as I busy myself in the kitchen. Hunter's gifts are nestled under the tree, and I quickly fill his stocking. Seeing how much effort he put into making the place look great last night after I feel asleep, just warms my heart.

The coffee machine is brewing Hunter's favorite morning pick-me-up, and I'm going to add a sprinkle of cinnamon to the froth on top. If I could do those cool designs you get in a coffeehouse, I'd draw him a love heart. The last time I tried, it looked like a ball sack, and he didn't exactly find that enticing.

I call my mom and dad to wish them a Merry Christmas, which is a brief conversation this year, and then I call my brother. Next on my list is Zee.

"Merry Christmas, bestie!" I'm a tad overexuberant for the time of day, but Zee's used to it.

"Merry Christmas. How are you so peppy? It's still dark out."

"It's Christmas. What's not to be peppy about? My husband is sound asleep in the matching festive onesie I bought for him, I'm making cinnamon rolls, and my best friend in the whole world is coming over to share Christmas dinner with me. I'd say I have plenty to be ecstatic about this year."

"Bully for you."

"What's wrong?"

"Nothing. I'm just tired."

"Up all night helping Coop get rid of the butt plug?"

"He's not here."

"What? Did y'all have a fight?"

"We're not married, Faith. I have to go see my folks this morning before I come over to your place, or I'll never hear the end of it. Cooper has family obligations as well. We're not at the stage where we're ready to meet each other's families. No biggy. He'll be at your place later, so I'll see him there."

"Why do I feel like you're spinning me a load of bullshit right now?"

"I don't know. Everything is peachy. Can we change the subject? Has your electricity meter exploded yet? I can see the light coming off your place from way across town."

"Very funny. My home is bathed in the warm glow of Christmas magicalness."

"That's not even a word."

"It is in my world."

"So, I'm going to go see my folks once I get off the phone with you, spend a few hours there and grab a light lunch, then I'll head your way. Is there anything I need to bring other than my sparkling wit and incredibly good looks?"

"Some humility," I say with a chuckle.

"No can do, friend. Have you met me? I'm freaking awesome."

"I can't argue with that. See you soon and drive safe, the roads look icy."

"Yes, ma'am."

When I hang up the phone, a pang of worry blooms in my stomach. I need to sit down sometime soon and have a proper conversation with Zee about where she and Coop are at.

I go back to Christmas tunes and baking until eight o'clock. I can't wait any longer, so I pour Hunter a coffee, make him a plate of cinnamon rolls, and head for our bedroom. Balancing his plate on top of the coffee mug, I reach for the lamp on the nightstand, but his breakfast starts to slide off the plate. He wakes with a start and grabs the mug without even opening his eyes.

"Fuck!"

I jump back, sending the cinnamon rolls flying, but at least the coffee didn't spill. I could've just permanently scarred my husband with a nasty burn.

"Oh God! I'm sorry. I didn't mean to startle you. I just wanted to bring you breakfast in bed."

"Faith, please *never* lean over me with a scalding hot cup of coffee. I love you, but you can't be trusted not to burn my nuts off. Now, grab me a cinnamon roll off the floor."

"I'll go and get you a fresh plate."

"They're fine. Five second rule... or more like a fifteen second rule in this case." He leans over the bed and grabs one of the rolls off the floor, shoving the entire thing in his mouth in one go. "Tasty."

"Merry Christmas, Hunter."

"Merry Christmas, love." Crumbs come flying out of his mouth.

"Say it, don't spray it!" He pulls me close, wrapping his arms tight around me.

"Are you ready to go open gifts?"

"I was ready two hours ago! Thank you for wearing the PJs, it made me so happy when I woke up this morning." He rolls his eyes at me, but I know he's digging them. Otherwise, he just wouldn't have worn them. Not that I'd have been upset waking up next to a naked Hunter, but it feels super festive to match on our first Christmas together.

"Is this going to be one of our traditions?"

"Of course. And when we have kids, we can get those cute family sets. It'll be awesome." Hunter's entire body tenses.

"Kids? Do you want to have babies?" The color drains from his face.

"Do you?" It wasn't a conscious thought when I said it. We haven't ever talked about it.

"Sure, but not right now. I want some time with you when it's just us. Everything this year has been warp speed, but this isn't one of those things… right?"

"I totally agree. I'm in no rush to burst my vagina giving birth. I'm talking way, way… way down the line." There's an audible sigh of relief from Hunter.

"Okay. You scared the shit out of me for a minute there."

"Is the thought of having babies with me so terrible?" I'm just playing with him, but his expression sobers.

"Of course not."

"You're worried my DNA would produce sons who couldn't run a football field without injury, aren't you? Or daughters who have all the grace and poise of a rhinoceros? Or worse, kids who make dumbass wagers with people?"

"Well, when you put it like that, maybe we should consider how much carnage your DNA could cause in the world." I shove his shoulder, faking upset.

"It must be great to be you. Athletic, sexy, coordinated!"

"It's pretty awesome. I snagged myself a hot wife who's completely out of my league, but I guess she found my coordination irresistible." I definitely find him irresistible.

"Can we go open presents now?" I bounce on the bed, straddling him. "Let's go already!"

"Bouncing your perfect little ass on my junk isn't going to speed up this process. If anything, I might just grab some tinsel and tie you to the bed. Then I could have my wicked way with you all day long. Now, that sounds like a perfect Christmas."

"No getting naked until after presents."

"That's all the gift I need. I can see you're about to explode if we don't get this show on the road, so come on, Mrs. Vaughn, let's go and see what's under the tree."

I practically drag Hunter down the hallway to the living room and immediately grab my phone.

"First Christmas selfie."

"You're not taking a picture of me in this onesie." There's no conviction in his voice. He's definitely resigned to this being next year's holiday card.

"I already took a picture of you curled up in bed asleep this morning looking super adorable in your PJs."

"Creepy. Do you often take pictures of me in my sleep?"

"A true creeper never tells." I snuggle close at his side and snap a pic of us.

I love giving gifts more than I enjoy receiving them. Some of the presents I bought for Hunter were silly little things, but every item I picked out for him had meaning. Other gifts were sentimental and sappy, but he got such a kick out of everything. I knew during our festive wager that Hunter has a softer side. He gave each of us some heartfelt gifts. Nothing embarrassing or devious—he left that to the rest of us or, more aptly, me.

When our living room looks like a bomb filled with wrapping paper went off in it, I sit back and take it all in. I don't want to forget a single moment of this Christmas with Hunter. I'm looking forward to dinner with Coop and Zee, but until then, I plan to unwrap the best gift I got this year—Hunter.

"You've got that devious look on your face. What are you thinking?"

"We have a gorgeous Christmas tree and a warm fire. It only seems right that we celebrate our first Christmas with a bang. *A naked bang!*"

"Now that's a tradition I can get behind."

We lose ourselves in a tangle of passionate kisses and a slow sensual fuck. I will never tire of Hunter making love to me. I'll always cherish his kiss and worship his body with everything that I am.

"They're here!"

After a wonderful first half of the day, I'm looking forward to sharing the evening with our friends.

Dinner is almost ready, and the house smells like Christmas. I throw open the door and pull my best friend into my arms. "Merry Christmas!"

Coop stands patiently while we hug it out. When Zee finally lets go of me and heads inside, I pull him close.

"Merry Christmas, Faith."

"Merry Christmas, Coop. Come in, come in. I have mountains of food and gifts for y'all."

"Please tell me it's not another butt plug. I'm still hurting today."

"Not another plug. I got you lube to go with the one you have." Hunter appears at my side, coming to greet his best friend.

"Don't wind him up. No one can tell when you're joking now. Not after your antics this holiday season."

"Only good gifts. I promise. Nothing that's meant for any orifice of the body. Cross my heart."

"Thank fuck for that."

Coop and Hunter give each other their customary bromance version of a hug, slapping each other on the back.

"Merry Christmas, bro. I've got a bottle of scotch with our name on it."

"Sounds like a plan."

Laughter fills the air as we enjoy celebrating with our friends. The boys kick back with a few drinks while Zee sits at the kitchen island chatting with me as I prepare a feast fit for a king.

When we sit down to dinner, my heart is full of joy. Hunter and Coop keep us laughing, regaling us with stories of Christmases past with the Titans. Every now and again, I catch Zee staring at Coop, hanging on his every word. My hope for the coming new year is that they find their way together. I know it's idealistic to wish for my best friend to fall in love with my husband's best friend, but they are great together.

"Time to fess up." Coop pins me with his stare. "Let's find out the identity of our Secret Santa gifts."

"Why are you looking at me?" I feign innocence, but everyone at this table knows me too well to believe me.

"I know you were responsible for my ruination."

"Sorry, Coop."

He sits back, crossing his arms over his chest with a hearty chuckle.

"If you'd done it to Vaughn, I'd have had a field day with it. It's all good. Last night I wasn't exactly thrilled about it, but today, I can see the funny side."

"Who sent me the sexy elf outfit?" Zee looks to Coop, expecting him to be the culprit.

"That would also be me."

"I did *not* see that coming!" Zee shoves me. "Witch."

"Sorry, bestie. If it's any consolation, you really were smoking hot in it."

"Of course, I was. I'd be hot as a trash bag."

"Okay. So, we know the gifts I sent. Who sent me the vibrating underwear?"

Coop sheepishly raises his hand. Hunter is about to lay into him when I reach under the table and squeeze his thigh.

"I for sure thought it was Zee."

"Bro, I really want to sucker-punch you right now. And why the fuck didn't you switch the damn thing off after Faith totaled the table?"

"The remote fell on the floor. I couldn't find it in amongst the mess, and I guess it got dumped by the waitstaff when they cleaned up."

"So, some waiter was clicking the buttons. Fucking hell." Hunter is about to pop a vein in his forehead just thinking about it.

"Baby, does it really matter now? We ended up having ridiculously hot sex, so it's all good."

"Mmm… not sure I agree with that."

"Who sent Hunter the suitcase and penis pump?"

"My guess is Coop." Hunter thought it was him from the get-go.

"That was my brainchild." I'm speechless as Zee admits to sending them.

I burst out laughing. "No way. That was epic. High-five, bestie. I never would've thought to photoshop a whole ad. Love it."

"What did I ever do you to you?" Hunter jokes.

"You married my soulmate. You get her, you get me. Sorry, Hunter, you're stuck with me. I promise there will be no more penis pumps unless you need one."

"Fuck that. My cock is good as is, thank you very much."

"Yeah, yeah. We know. You're so manly." Zee loves winding him up, and it warms my heart to see them getting along so well. I don't know what I'd do if they didn't like each other. It doesn't bear thinking about.

"Now that we know who did all the embarrassing gifts, let's move on to the good ones. Who sent what?" Coop asks, adjusting the new Rolex on his wrist—one of his anonymous presents.

"That's an easy one. None of you fuckers sent anything resembling a nice gift. I sent all of them. I know that makes me boring, but I wanted to give you guys something personal, things I thought you'd actually enjoy."

"I think my ovaries just exploded." I knew all those 'secret' presents were from Hunter, but hearing him say it out loud makes me weak at the knees.

"Holy shit. I'm seriously lost for words right now." Zee stands from the table, walks over to Hunter, and throws her arms around his neck. "Thank you."

"You're welcome. We're family now. If I'm stuck with you, you're stuck with me."

"Deal."

The rest of the night is full of fun and games—literally. It's not Christmas without a good game to play after dinner. Card Against Humanity paired with a healthy dose of alcohol makes for a very amusing evening. Come the end of the night, we're all stuffed from eating way too much and exhausted from an eventful festive season. The conversation is easy, and the laughs are constant.

"It's getting late, we should leave you guys to it." Zee pulls out her phone to call a cab, but I grab it out of her hand before she gets the chance.

"You can stay here."

"Only if you're sure?"

"Of course. I wouldn't have it any other way." Zee wraps her arm around me, leaning her head on my shoulder.

"Good, cause it's fucking freezing outside, and my apartment is probably a block of ice right about now."

"Then, it's settled. You guys can crash here, and then you'll be able to help us eat all the leftovers tomorrow."

"We're going to have to start paying rent here soon," Coop says as he interlaces his fingers with Zee's. "Thank you for inviting us to spend Christmas with you guys. I know it's your first holiday together, and I just want you to know that I appreciate you including us... me... us."

"Our door is always open... holidays, weekdays, Sundays. If it ends with 'day,' then you're welcome here."

"I'm starting to feel the effects of all that scotch. I might call it a night." He turns his attention to Zee. "Are you staying up, or do you want to come to bed with me?"

All of a sudden, I feel like Hunter and I are intruding on an intimate moment. It's not what he said, but the way he said it—laced with desire and the promise of anything but sleep.

Without a word, Zee stands, leading Coop to the staircase, their eyes fixed on one another. Hunter and I cease to exist in their world, and the moment they disappear upstairs to the guest room, Hunter takes my hand and pulls me over to the couch, sitting me down.

"I should really clear the dishes."

"They can wait until tomorrow. I have one last gift for you, Faith. Wait here." He disappears for a minute and returns holding a large rectangular present. "This year has been so amazing, and I wanted to make sure we remember it in years to come."

"What is it?" He puts the beautifully wrapped gift in my lap.

"Open it."

"Come sit down with me." He takes a seat next to me, eager to gauge my reaction. I wonder what has him a little unsure of himself. I pull the ribbon and rip open the paper. Whatever is inside, I'm already impressed with the box. Our names are embossed on the lid in gold script.

"Open it. I'm dying over here."

"Why are you nervous? I don't think I've ever seen you show any kind of nerves before." He reaches over and plants a soft kiss on my lips.

"I put a lot of thought into it, and I'm just worried you'll think it's corny." Now I'm intrigued.

Removing the lid carefully, I pull back the tissue paper to find a photo book. There's a picture of us on the front I've never seen before. It's from the Hall of Fame when Hunter proposed. Someone captured a shot of him down on one knee, staring up at me with adoration in his eyes. I haven't even opened it, and I'm ready to start crying.

I take a moment to compose myself before flipping the page. I'm expecting pictures of us, maybe from the wedding or other events where people take a lot of photos. What I'm seeing, page after page, aren't our public moments. Hunter isn't even in most of the pictures.

Each page has been crafted so beautifully, the same way our wedding album was, with stylish-framed photographs with captions next to each one—they are all candid pictures of me. I study page after page, reading Hunter's words and connecting the dots. These are all pictures Hunter has taken of me when I didn't know he was watching.

His words are so heartfelt, telling a story of our journey this year. There are so many pictures before we were officially a couple. Days and events I remember going back to right after I challenged Hunter to the wager that brought us together.

Looking at this incredible gift, I see a different side of our relationship in those early days—even before we *had* a relationship to speak of.

"I can't believe you did this. You took all of these photos? Why?" I point to a shot of me from the charity day Hunter trained with a whole field of kids. We were nothing more than a flirtation back then, or so I thought. I knew I felt more than I should for him, even when I insisted he'd be no more than a pleasure transaction.

"From the moment you came fumbling into my life, I knew you could never just be a fling. Every day I watched you, entranced by your beauty and infectious personality. I couldn't get enough of you. It was in those quiet moments when you weren't aware of my gaze that I fell head over heels in love with you… long before I thought you could ever reciprocate those feelings. I guess this is my way of letting you see yourself through my eyes."

"Hunter. It's so beautiful."

"You know I find your lack of coordination endearing, and I know we joke about it a lot, but I wanted you to see that there's so much more to you. You have a grace and elegance of spirit that floors me and has me waking up every morning feeling like the luckiest guy on the planet that I get to share this life with you. We're our own little family now, and your love is the greatest gift I'll ever receive. I love you."

I launch myself into his arms, my lips crashing down on his in a fierce kiss.

"I love you, Hunter Vaughn. Merry Christmas."

"Merry Christmas, Faith. My stunning wife, partner in crime, and forever my Lady Fumble."

The End
Merry Christmas!
BUY COOP AND ZEE'S BOOK INTERCEPTION TODAY
SIGN UP FOR EVA'S NEWSLETTER

Acknowledgments

This year as been tough on everyone, and this series has been an outlet for me when I needed it most. Discovering a love for writing romantic comedy has been such a gift in a difficult year. Simon, thank you so much for encouraging me to lose my anxieties in a world of my own creation. I love you more than words could say.

Ria, you know this book was never meant to be. A whim that came to mind and I just couldn't resist delving back into Faith and Hunter's shenanigans. Thank you for not thinking I was crazy for giving myself more work, and for championing me every step of the way. I love you more!

Thank you to my editor, Nicki Kuzn. Your hard work is always appreciated, and I know when I get a comment on my edits that you couldn't stop laughing, I must be doing something right. I look forward to the many projects we will be working on together in 2021.

To my readers, old and new, thank you. The outpouring of love for FUMBLE and these characters has been truly overwhelming for me. I never thought Faith and Hunter would get to sit side by side next to comedy legends like Trevor Noah, and Jerry Seinfeld in the Amazon charts. It's a dream come true and it is all because of you. Thank you so much. I hope you enjoy spending the holidays with the Vaughns!

About the Author

I'm happiest when wandering through the uncharted territory of my imagination. You'll find me curled up with my laptop, browsing the books at the local library, or enjoying the smell of a new book, taking great delight in cracking the spine and writing in the margins!

Eva is a native Scot but lives in Texas with her husband, two kids, and a whizzy little fur baby with the most ridiculous ears. She first fell in love with British literature while majoring in Linguistics, 17th Century Poetry, and Shakespeare at University. She is an avid reader and lifelong notebook hoarder. In 2014, she finally put her extensive collection to good use and started writing her first novel. Previously published with Prism Heart Press under a pen name, Eva decided to branch out on her own and lend her name to her full back catalogue! She is currently working on some exciting new projects.

Social Media

www.instagram.com/evahainingauthor

www.facebook.com/evahainingauthor

www.twitter.com/evahaining

www.amazon.com/author/evahaining

www.bookbub.com/profile/eva-haining

https://www.goodreads.com/author/show/20271110.Eva_Haining

www.evahaining.com

Made in the USA
Coppell, TX
27 September 2024

37799290R00059